"Don't You Ever Wonder?"

"Wonder what?" she asked, her voice that husky whisper that did crazy things to him.

"What it will be like when we kiss again."

"Who said we'll kiss again?"

"Oh, we will. Don't you want to know if what happened the first time will happen again? Whether we could be *that* good, again?"

She blinked and drew in a breath, the word *no* beginning to form on her lips. The sound never made it out as he closed the short distance between them, caressing her lips with his.

The sensation that shuddered through his body was intense. Even more potent than the last time. He stepped closer, aligning his body with hers. She met his assault with a parry of her own, clinging to him.

His need to possess her overwhelmed everything else—every need, every thought, other than one. He wanted Anna Garrick like he'd never wanted anything in his life before.

* * *

Dear Reader,

Once again a historical home has inspired a story idea—well, in this case, multiple story ideas.

I had the great good fortune to be invited to speak at the South Australian Romance Authors one-day workshop in May of 2010, and in the days afterward I was shown some of the stunning countryside through the Adelaide Hills and beyond. During the workshop day, one of the attendees, a marriage celebrant, was telling us about one of the most interesting weddings she'd conducted in the ruins of a gothic mansion high on the hills. I didn't have time to actually visit the ruins at Marble Hill, but I did spend a lot of time on their website fascinated by the building, its destruction and the current plans to rebuild it to its former glory. A spark of an idea formed.

With my mind ticking away, I had the additional brain power of my good friend Trish Morey to storm up some ideas, and by the time I arrived home those ideas began to morph into this new miniseries, starting with *The Wayward Son* and continuing next month with *A Forbidden Affair.*

In many ways creating the backstory of these books was just as fascinating as creating the books themselves, and I look forward to bringing you more of The Master Vintners in coming years.

Happy reading!

Yvonne Lindsay

YVONNE LINDSAY

THE WAYWARD SON

Recycling programs
for this product may
not exist in your area.

ISBN-13: 978-0-373-73154-1

THE WAYWARD SON

Copyright © 2012 by Dolce Vita Trust

www.Harlequin.com

Printed in U.S.A.

Recent books by Yvonne Lindsay

Harlequin Desire

Bought: His Temporary Fiancée #2078
The Pregnancy Contract #2117
††*The Wayward Son* #2141

Silhouette Desire

**The Boss's Christmas Seduction* #1758
**The CEO's Contract Bride* #1776
**The Tycoon's Hidden Heir* #1788
Rossellini's Revenge Affair #1811
Tycoon's Valentine Vendetta #1854
Jealousy & A Jewelled Proposition #1873
Claiming His Runaway Bride #1890
†*Convenient Marriage, Inconvenient Husband* #1923
†*Secret Baby, Public Affair* #1930
†*Pretend Mistress, Bona Fide Boss* #1937
Defiant Mistress, Ruthless Millionaire #1986
***Honor-Bound Groom* #2029
***Stand-In Bride's Seduction* #2038
***For the Sake of the Secret Child* #2044

*New Zealand Knights
†Rogue Diamonds
**Wed at Any Price
††The Master Vintners

Other titles by this author available in ebook format

YVONNE LINDSAY

New Zealand born, to Dutch immigrant parents, Yvonne Lindsay became an avid romance reader at the age of thirteen. Now, married to her "blind date" and with two fabulous children, she remains a firm believer in the power of romance. Yvonne feels privileged to be able to bring to her readers the stories of her heart. In her spare time, when not writing, she can be found with her nose firmly in a book, reliving the power of love in all walks of life. She can be contacted via her website, www.yvonnelindsay.com.

To E.M.
—In the immortal words of Casper, "Can I keep you?"

One

She hadn't seen anything quite this beautiful in forever. The exquisitely colored autumnal landscape aside, the figure of the man chopping wood in the distance, shirt off, muscles rippling in the still-warm Adelaide Hills sunshine, was quite enough to remind Anna of every hormonal response her body was capable of. And then some.

Never averse to indulging in appreciation of the male form—even if her busy work-filled schedule meant she rarely did anything about it—she walked a little closer. A tingle of awareness skimmed across her skin, raising goose bumps on the surface, which had nothing to do with the hint of evening breeze that rolled through the hills. It was only when she was about twenty meters from him that recognition hit her with all the subtlety of a bucket of ice water.

Judd Wilson.

Her entire reason for being in Australia.

Although they'd never met, there was no mistaking Charles Wilson's son. Obviously tall, Judd had dark hair and warmly

tanned skin stretched over a physique that was the epitome of
every woman's fantasy. His sharply sculpted features hinted
at a resemblance to his father. She'd hazard a guess his eyes
were the same piercing blue, as well.

Anna was surprised when her inner muscles clenched on
a purely instinctive female reaction and her heart stuttered
a little in her chest. She hadn't responded this strongly to
anyone in a while, and she sure as hell never expected to
feel so drawn to the son of the man who was not only her
employer, but practically a father to her. She drew in a deep
breath and forced back the flood of attraction that threatened
to swamp her anew—reminding herself that she was here on
business. She'd made a promise to Charles—a promise she
fully intended to keep.

His instructions had been painfully clear. Somehow she
had to persuade Judd Wilson to come home to New Zealand,
before the father he hadn't seen in more than two decades
died.

Anna took a few more tentative steps through the path-
way designated amongst the rows and rows of grapevines
that striated the land. Her eyes were fixed on the male figure
working ahead of her—the man completely oblivious to the
bombshell she was about to drop on his world. She paused
for a moment, sudden nerves weakening her resolve.

Judd had been only six years old when his parents' divorce
resulted in his and his mother's leaving New Zealand—not
to mention leaving Charles, and Judd's baby sister, Nicole—
behind for good. Did he even remember his father? Would
he be pleased at the chance to reconcile, or would he be bitter
over all the lost years?

Anxiety over Judd's potential reaction was swiftly followed by a swirl of familiar anger and defensiveness on
Charles's behalf. If it hadn't been for Cynthia Masters-
Wilson's deceptions, Charles would never have been separated from his son in the first place. Anna hadn't yet met the

woman who had torn apart Charles's very reasons for existence, and she certainly wasn't looking forward to it. No doubt it would prove to be a necessary evil at some stage, but for now her focus was on meeting Charles's son and on gauging what his response to his father's contact would be. Her intense physical reaction to him now promised to make that a little more complicated than Anna had anticipated.

She was here with a job to do, she reminded herself sternly, even as her eyes flicked back toward Judd's sun-kissed torso one more time. She couldn't afford to let herself get distracted. Perhaps right now was not the best time to meet him and try to broach the topic. This was a matter that would require good timing and not a small amount of finesse if she was to be successful, and she owed it to Charles to be successful. Lord only knew he'd done more than enough for her family over the years. The least she could do in return was bring some peace of mind to the man who had supported Anna and her late mother for most of Anna's life. She couldn't just barge in and potentially destroy her one opportunity to bring Judd Wilson home.

She took a turn in a different direction, determined now to create some distance between herself and the very man she'd flown almost five hours to see. There would be time enough during her stay here at The Masters' Vineyard and Accommodation, she reasoned with herself. She had to tread this road very carefully if she was going to succeed.

Despite her best intentions, she didn't get very far.

"Hi, there," a voice as rich and sensual as a classic Shiraz called out from behind her. "It's a beautiful evening, isn't it?"

She couldn't ignore him now—not when it was vital she make a good impression. Anna braced herself as she turned around to face her boss's son.

Must be the new guest for the accommodation side of the business, Judd thought to himself as he watched the woman come closer. His cousin Tamsyn sent an update to all staff at the vineyard at the beginning of each week as to which of the luxurious cottages on the property would be accommodating guests for the coming days. She certainly hadn't mentioned that their newest visitor was so stunning.

Judd narrowed his eyes and tracked the movements of the woman in the blue dress as she approached. She walked with a gracefulness that belied the uneven ground she strolled along, and there was a sensual sway to her hips that sent a jolt of pure male appreciation rocketing through his body.

"Judd Wilson, welcome to The Masters'." Judd shifted the ax to his left hand so he could reach out his right to shake. She smiled in response, a slow movement of her lips that made his groin tighten almost imperceptibly, but the effect when she placed her hand in his was unmistakable. Raw need, hot and greedy, unfurled with latent intent. Interesting. Very interesting. Perhaps he'd found a solution to the boredom that had been plaguing him for weeks. He smiled back and clasped her hand firmly.

"Hi, I'm Anna Garrick," she said, her voice husky.

Her eyes searched his face keenly. As if she was looking for something. Perhaps some spark of recognition from him? No, the instant he thought of it, he eschewed the idea. If he'd ever met Anna Garrick before, he had no doubt he'd have remembered her.

From the top of her burnished dark chestnut-colored hair to her perfectly proportioned body and the tips of her painted toenails, she was his every fantasy. Even her voice—slightly soft, slightly rough—stroked his senses in a way he could never forget.

"Lovely to meet you, Anna. Did you arrive today?"

Her eyes flicked away, as if she was suddenly nervous— or hiding something. Judd felt his instincts go on alert.

"Yes, I did. It's wonderful here. You're so lucky to live in such a beautiful area. Have you…worked here long?" The question was innocent, but he'd caught the slight hesitation, as if she'd started out with the intention of asking something else.

"You could say that," Judd replied, his smile tightening. "It's something of a Masters family business—I grew up here."

"But your name…"

Ah, yes, his name. The reminder of the father who cast him aside all those years ago—and the reason why, even as the very successful head of The Masters' far-flung interests, some of his cousins still never quite treated him like he belonged.

"My mother is Cynthia Masters-Wilson," he replied. No need to go into details. Not when there were so many more pleasurable things he'd like to discuss with this woman.

"And do all Masters chop wood for the winery fireplaces?" she teased.

"But of course," he replied in kind. "Anything at all we can do to make your stay more…pleasurable." That certainly sounded better than admitting that he'd needed the tension release after an incredibly frustrating day of work.

Some days were like that. Bashing at the keys on a laptop didn't quite cut it when you just needed to get physical. And when his choices were either to chop wood or to resort to physical violence against his cousin Ethan, Judd had, reluctantly, chosen chopping wood.

Of course, Ethan really did need someone to knock his head straight. The man might run the winemaking side of the business with undeniable skill—their stock of award-winning wines was proof enough of that—but he was so stuck in his ways, he might as well be cemented in place. Ethan was devoted to maintaining the integrity and superiority of the wines that were synonymous with The Masters' brand. With the current glut of certain wine varieties on the local market, Judd was equally adamant that Ethan needed to diversify. He'd been suggesting it from the day the first projections about the excesses had arisen some years ago. His cousin was like a bear with a sore head on the issue and even more stubborn with it.

Yes, he definitely needed the distraction Ms. Garrick provided.

"And I do hope you'll let me know if there's anything at all *I* can do for you," he added.

"I'll keep that in mind," she replied. "But I can't think of anything I need at the moment. My plan for now is just to enjoy a ramble through these lovely grounds before it gets too dark."

"Then I'll let you return to it. But I'll be seeing you at dinner tonight?"

"Dinner?"

"Yes, we have a family dinner to welcome the new guests every week. There would have been an invitation in your welcome pack when you checked in. It begins with drinks in the formal sitting room of the main house at seven o'clock." Judd stepped closer, taking hold of her hand again. "You will be there, won't you?"

"Yes, I'd like that."

"Excellent," he murmured. "Until then." He lifted her hand, brushing his lips against the back in a soft kiss. She seemed taken aback for a moment, but then she gave him another slow, delicious smile before walking away. Judd leaned on the ax handle and watched her go. Shadows were beginning to creep along the foothills. He looked up to the ruins of the gothic mansion that crowned the nearby peak.

The charred remains were all that was left of the original Masters home. Years after its destruction, it remained a symbol of the family's past glory and their fight to rebuild a world that had been burned to the ground in a devastating sweep of ravenous bushfire. You had to admire a family that had had every marker of their wealth laid to waste, but who had fought back, tooth and nail, to be where they were today.

He was proud to be a part of that heritage. Despite his name, he was as much a Masters as any one of his many cousins and had just as much right to be here. Even so, he'd always felt as if he was an outsider. It had made him work twice as hard to prove his worth, and that work ethic had pushed The Masters' forward and onto a global platform beyond the family's expectations since he'd taken over as head of operations.

But perhaps he'd been too work-focused lately. It had been a while since he'd let loose. His duties here had consumed him for months now. Today, he'd finally admitted to himself that, no matter how hard he pushed himself, he was bored. Life, work, everything lacked the challenge he craved. A little light flirtation with the lovely Anna Garrick could be the perfect antithesis to the frustrations he was facing.

Judd methodically stacked the pile of logs he'd split and put away his tools before heading for his suite of rooms and having a much-needed shower. The prospect of another evening with his family suddenly held a great deal more appeal than it had after his latest altercation with Ethan's inflexible attitude.

Perhaps he'd found the challenge he was seeking after all.

Judd's hair was still slightly damp when he made his way into the formal sitting room, where whichever members of the Masters clan who were resident gathered for drinks with the guests before dinner. It was an old-fashioned habit, one that had its roots firmly linked to the ruins on the hill and a lifestyle long since gone, but one which still held a certain charm and which had no doubt been integral in keeping the family so firmly knit together.

Sunset brought a deeper chill to the air outside, which was offset by the crackling fire in the large stone fireplace.

He cast a glance around the room, giving a grim-lipped nod briefly in Ethan's direction before smiling at his mother, who sat, with her usual supreme elegance, on one of the chairs near the fireplace. No sign of the new guest yet.

He crossed to the sideboard and poured himself a half glass of The Masters' pinot noir. As he did so, he saw the object of his intentions hover in the doorway. He moved toward her immediately, but his mother—ever vigilant—beat him there. As he approached, he could hear her questioning Anna.

"Excuse me for being so forward, but you do look familiar to me. Have you stayed here before?" Cynthia asked.

To his surprise, a swiftly masked look of shock flitted across Anna's face.

"N-no," she replied. "This is my first visit to South Australia, although I hope it won't be my last."

She smiled, but her eyes still held a shadow of the shock he'd seen earlier. Was she lying? His instincts honed to a sharper edge. Ms. Garrick was becoming very interesting indeed.

"Perhaps you have a double out there. They say we all do." Cynthia glossed over any awkwardness with an arch of one expertly plucked brow. "Tell me, what can Judd get you to drink, my dear?"

"A glass of sauvignon blanc would be lovely, thank you. I hear you recently were awarded two golds for your sauvs."

"Yes, we were. We're very proud of Ethan and what he's doing with the wines," Cynthia said with a pointed look toward her son that told Judd his cousin had probably already apprised her of their earlier dispute. "Aren't we, Judd?"

"He's a master, that's for sure," Judd agreed.

His double entendre didn't go unnoticed by his mother, who flung him a silent rebuke with her expressive eyes, before apparently deciding it would be a suitable punishment to him to lead Anna away and introduce her to the other members of the family. Judd was forced to admit that his mother had chosen her chastisement well—Anna was the only one in the room whose company he truly wanted tonight.

He stood with one hand in his trouser pocket and observed Anna's movements as she was introduced to Cynthia's two older brothers and then Ethan. The instant his cousin stood to welcome the newcomer, Judd's hackles rose and every feral instinct inside of him leaped to the fore.

Something must have shown on his face, because he didn't miss the spark of interest in Ethan's eye before his cousin leaned forward to say something to Anna. Something which made her laugh. The sound itself was enough to send his blood humming along his veins, but knowing it was Ethan who had brought that laugh to her delectable lips set his teeth on edge.

Determined not to give his cousin the satisfaction of knowing just how much, and how surprisingly, his action had riled him, Judd turned to welcome Ethan's sister, Tamsyn, as she appeared in the door.

"I see you've already met our latest guest," she commented, removing his untouched pinot noir from his hands and taking a sip. Her brand-new engagement ring flashed brilliantly in the overhead lights. "Mmm, good. Can you pour me one?"

"Have this one, I haven't touched it."

"Thanks," Tamsyn answered with a smile.

"That fiancé of yours not here with you tonight?"

"No, he's still in the city—working." Her warm brown eyes searched his face. "You look tense. Is everything okay?"

Judd forced a smile to his lips. Tamsyn always had the unerring ability to sense when something was wrong with him.

"Nothing that won't be sorted when your brother learns to pay as much attention to market trends as he does to our guests," he commented.

Tamsyn laughed. "Oh, well, good luck with that, cuz. You

know market trends are the last thing Ethan concerns himself with. But I wouldn't growl too much about that." She nodded in Anna's direction. "You know Ethan's partial to blondes. And this particular brunette keeps sneaking glances at you, anyway. Have you met her yet?"

Judd nodded, letting his gaze track back to Anna's slender form and drinking in the smooth lines of her body, allowing a satisfaction-filled smile to cross his face when he realized his cousin was right—Anna's attention wandered in his direction several times. "Did she say what she was doing here in Adelaide?"

"No, I just assumed it was a short vacation. She didn't say much when she rang to make the booking."

"A short vacation?"

"I'm sure you'll have plenty of time to get to know her," Tamsyn teased. "But yeah, she's only here four days."

"I'd better not let her waste any more of her time here, then," he replied. "If you'll excuse me."

Without waiting for Tamsyn's reply he made his way across the room and to Anna's side. She turned and gave him a smile.

"It must be lovely being able to work with your extended family like this," she said. "Ethan's been filling me in on what you all do."

"It has its benefits, certainly," Judd agreed. "Tell me, have you planned any extended sightseeing while you're here? As luck would have it, I find myself with a couple of days with little to do and I'd love to show you around if you're keen."

Anna told herself to remain calm. This was exactly the opportunity she needed. Time alone with Judd Wilson would help her to better find out what he was like. She knew Charles had expected her to simply make an appointment with him and to give him the letter that even now burned a hole in her evening bag, but despite Charles's directive, she wanted to understand her boss's son just a little more before she took that step. God only knew that Charles had borne his fair share of disappointment in his lifetime and, if she had her way, his last years would be quite the opposite.

As much as Charles longed to be reunited with Judd, Anna knew that Charles was braced for his son's refusal. That was why he'd told no one but Anna how crucial it was to him to bring Judd back into the fold. Charles had sworn her to complete secrecy, not allowing her to tell even his daughter, Nicole, who had subtly taken up the reins of the company when Charles first got sick, any of the details of this trip. The cone of silence rankled, especially when Nicole was her best friend and they all not only worked together, but lived under the same roof, as well. Anna couldn't help but feel that she was betraying Nicole by doing all of this behind her back.

It was for Charles's sake, she reminded herself. And Charles deserved her very best efforts to convince his son to come home. If only she knew what the best approach was for her to take!

Instinct told her that Judd might be more receptive if she hid her true purpose for a little while longer and got him to open up to her more before she revealed the truth of her visit. But the purely female part of her worried that the longer she put off her business, the harder it would be for her to resist the powerful draw pulling her toward him. She chose her response to Judd Wilson's suggestion carefully.

"Are you sure? I wouldn't want to impose on you. It's my first visit to the region and I can already tell I haven't left myself enough time to enjoy it fully."

Judd leaned in closer. "Maybe we can entice you to come back again."

His words sent a shiver of anticipation across her skin. If the man got any more enticing she'd need a chillingly cold shower before the night was through. This visceral reaction to Judd Wilson was an unexpected complication she wasn't quite sure how to handle. But at least his reply showed her one thing—he was *definitely* willing to let her get to know *him* better…at least for as long as she hid the truth.

A dinner bell sounded down the hall, saving her from making a response. Judd offered her his arm.

"May I escort you to the table?"

Anna hesitated a moment before tucking her hand in the crook of his arm. "Are you always this formal?" she asked.

He shot her a look, a fierce blue blaze of fire in his eyes that let her know in no uncertain terms that he himself could be very informal, indeed. Her body reacted on an unconscious level. Her nipples tightened, her breasts suddenly full and aching with a desire to be touched. Everything in her body tensed, drawing her into a heightened state of awareness.

"When I need to be," he responded with a smile that was pure wicked intent from the curve of his lips to the light that gleamed in his eyes.

Anna forced herself to break eye contact. The compelling power of his male beauty was quite enough to take her breath away and to addle her wits along with it. Maybe getting to know Judd Wilson wasn't such a good idea after all. As Charles's assistant, she had the opportunity to interact with many powerful and compelling men, but never before had she dealt with a man with such effortless charisma.

The next few days suddenly took on an edge of uncertainty. What on earth had she let herself in for?

Two

The long wooden table in the formal dining room had been set with a dazzling array of china, crystal and cutlery. Anna sent a silent prayer of thanks that her upbringing in Charles Wilson's home meant that such a setting didn't faze her. Charles had insisted she have all the same social advantages Nicole enjoyed, even if—with her mother's position as Charles's housekeeper and companion—she hadn't had anywhere near the same financial background.

Seated near the top of the table, at Judd's right, Anna could observe the family dynamics in action. It was clear that Cynthia was very much the female head of the household. If Judd Wilson physically resembled his father, his estranged sister, Nicole, was her mother personified.

Anna studied Cynthia from her vantage point at the table. This was what her friend would look like in another twenty-five years—without, perhaps, the faint lines of bitterness that bracketed the older woman's mouth. That said, and despite the swish of gray at her temples that contrasted to her thick, dark hair, Cynthia Masters-Wilson was still a striking woman.

She carried herself with an almost regal air—expecting everyone to defer to her wishes and not holding back her disapproval if those wishes were not observed. Anna wondered briefly what Cynthia had been like early in her marriage to Charles, and found herself caught by the older woman's very intent gaze. Giving her hostess a smile, Anna tore her eyes away, mildly horrified that she'd been caught staring. The last thing she wanted to do was attract attention to herself.

There was a strong bond between Cynthia and her son, too, Anna observed. Judd, it seemed, was the only one capable of defusing his mother's rather autocratic attitude and bringing a genuine smile of warmth to her fine features. So why then, when her son was obviously so important to her, had Cynthia left behind her one-year-old daughter, Nicole, when she'd returned to Australia? Had she ever taken a moment to think about the baby girl she'd left behind and what impact her abandonment would have on that infant's life?

Anna had come to Australia full of sympathy for Charles, who had been so hurt by Cynthia's actions during their marriage. But seeing the woman now just brought home how badly Nicole had been cheated, as well.

"You're looking serious. Is everything okay with your meal?" Judd asked softly in her ear.

The gentle caress of his warm breath made her skin tingle, and she forced her concentration back from where she'd let it lead her. Anna shook her head.

"No, everything is wonderful, thank you."

"Is it something else that's bothering you?" he pressed, reaching across the table in front of him to lift a bottle of wine to top off her glass.

Just you, she thought before giving her head a shake.

"I'm perhaps a little tired, that's all."

"We can be a bit overwhelming, can't we?" he commented.

"No, it's not that. Actually, I envy you this. I'm an only child, as were both my parents. To have so many family members all in one place... Well, you're lucky."

"Yes, we are lucky—and equally cursed at the same time," he said with a charming wink that took the sting out of the latter part of his statement.

And Nicole should have had the chance to be a part of this, too, Anna added silently. Not for the first time, she wondered what had happened to drive Charles and Cynthia, and their children, apart. Whatever it was, Charles had flatly refused to discuss it, aside from saying that Cynthia had betrayed his trust—something she knew that Charles considered unforgivable. Whatever it was, Anna knew that it had not only ruined his marriage, but it had led to a major rift between himself and his business partner also. So many lives altered. And here she was, trying to mend a fence. Boy, was she ever out of her depth.

By the time the meal had progressed to coffee and dessert, Anna asked to be excused from the table, pleading tiredness. The gentlemen at the table stood as she moved her chair back, and she found herself completely charmed by the effortless old-world manners.

"Thank you all so much for your company tonight, and for dinner," she said.

"You're very welcome, Anna. Just let housekeeping know tomorrow if you'll be joining us again during your stay," Cynthia said graciously. "Do you have anything special planned for tomorrow?"

"We'll be doing some sightseeing and then I'm taking her into Hahndorf for lunch," Judd interjected.

"Oh?"

Cynthia hid her surprise but not before giving her son a sharp look that gave Anna no doubt that his mother would be grilling him on his choice of companion the minute she left the room. Cynthia composed her features into a bland smile. "Well, then, I hope you enjoy our little taste of Germany. Sleep well."

"Thank you," Anna replied and turned to leave the room.

To her surprise, Judd followed her. As they reached the front door she stopped.

"Why did you tell your mother you're taking me out tomorrow?"

"Because I am," he said confidently. "You can't visit the Adelaide Hills without stopping at Hahndorf, as well. It would be culturally insensitive."

"Culturally insensitive or not, I got the impression she wasn't too pleased about it."

"She thinks I don't work hard enough, but that's my problem, not yours."

He opened the front door and gestured for her to precede him. Out on the narrow road that led to the restored pioneer's cottage where she was staying, Anna felt the night air close in around her with its frigid arms. She shivered, wishing she'd thought to bring her pashmina with her when she'd come across to the house earlier.

"At the risk of being cliché," Judd said, removing his dinner jacket and dropping it over her shoulders, "I think you need this more than I do."

"Thank you," she said softly.

He wasn't kidding. Judging by the heat of his body still held in the lining of his jacket, he certainly had no need of the garment. She instantly felt warmed by it. A faint waft of spice, blended intrinsically with a hint of vanilla and woody notes, enveloped her. She recognized the scent as Judd's cologne and felt her bones begin to melt.

"The nights can be quite cool here from now on. The staff will have lit the fire in your cottage for you. It should be lovely and warm compared to out here."

Anna had an instant and vivid flashback to watching Judd

chopping wood this afternoon. Did he accomplish everything with that much vigor?

"It's still a beautiful night," she said, looking upward at the inky darkness of the sky peppered with dots of light—anything to distract her from the influence of what he did to her.

"Certainly is."

There was something about his voice that made her drop her gaze and meet his. He was looking straight at her. Despite the fact that at least a meter separated them, she felt as if he'd reached out and touched her. Anna swallowed against the sudden dryness that parched her throat. This man was sensuality personified. With only one look, he had her virtually a quivering mess of longing.

She barely knew him and yet she was already on the verge of casting all her careful self-imposed rules to the four corners of the earth and inviting him to explore this overwhelming attraction between them. And she knew her feelings were reciprocated. She could feel the energy and tension fairly vibrating off him. What would he be like when he lost control, she wondered, allowing herself to dwell for only a moment on the idea before slamming it back behind her all too weak defenses.

She broke eye contact before she could do something totally out of character, and began to walk a little more briskly along the path. Judd silently kept pace with her. At the cottage, he waited as she opened the front door. She shrugged off his coat and handed it to him.

"Thank you again."

"You're welcome," he replied.

Why didn't he just turn and go? She felt a flush rise in her cheeks. Did he expect her to invite him in? The cottage came with both a well-stocked kitchen and wet bar complete with a wine chiller, she'd noticed on checking in earlier today. But what kind of message would that send, she wondered, if she asked him to join her for coffee, or a drink? One thing she knew for certain was where it would *lead*—straight to the luxuriously appointed bedroom, and a steamier, wilder night than any she'd had in years.

The thought aroused her as much as it scared her. She wasn't the kind of woman who hopped in bed with a man she'd barely met, and she'd never mixed business and pleasure before in her life. If she gave in to Judd's advances now, where would it leave her when she had to tell him the truth about why she was here?

"You're thinking again," Judd said, his lips twitching with a barest hint of a smile.

"I do that a lot," she admitted.

"Here, think on this, then."

Somehow he'd closed the distance between them without her noticing. His hand snaked around the back of her neck— his fingers warm against her cooler skin. Her face automatically tilted up toward his, her lips parting on a silent protest. She knew the protest was futile. She wanted this as much as he did, and she was helpless to ignore the demand.

His mouth, when it captured hers, was gentle, coaxing, and Anna felt as if he'd lit a fire that ran through her veins. A small part of her had hoped his kiss would be disappointing— something that would make it easier to refuse his attentions. In all honesty, she had known to the depths of her soul that his touch would be like this—*magic*—and she wanted that magic with every cell in her body.

She fisted her hands at her sides in an effort to prevent herself from reaching out and touching him. It would be too much, too difficult to step away from, but the way his lips teased hers invited her closer, and before she knew it, her hands were pressed against his chest, the fiery warmth of his skin burning through the expensive cotton of his shirt and letting her know that he could set other hidden parts of her aflame if only she'd let him.

His chest muscles shifted beneath her hands as he lifted his other arm to curve around her waist, drawing her closer to him. Hip to hip, there was no denying he was as powerfully aroused as she. Tension built in her body, coiling tight as he deepened their kiss and coaxed her lips open with his probing tongue.

He tasted of fine wine and illicit, unspoken promises. Promises that made her clench her thighs together against the swell of desire that rippled through her body before centering at the core of her belly. She rocked her pelvis against him, the movement a futile attempt to assuage the pressure building inside of her. Instead, it only incited her further. Anna kissed him back with a passion she'd never unleashed before, meeting his tongue with her own, letting him know that she was no innocent bystander in this assault on her senses.

She lifted her hands from his chest, sliding them upward, over his shoulders and the strong column of his neck, and burrowed her fingers in his dark hair, holding him to her as his lips devoured hers, as hers did his. She pressed her body against him, her nipples taut and sensitive against the lace of her bra, her breasts aching for his touch.

The call of a night bird punctuated the air, its unfamiliar sound bringing Anna back to her surroundings. Bringing her mind back to the task she'd been sent here to execute.

She untangled her fingers from Judd's hair, and let her hands drop to her sides once more. Their kiss, when it ended, was more bittersweet than she'd imagined, the loss of his caress felt deep inside. Judd rested his forehead against hers, his eyes still closed, his lips moist and slightly parted on an uneven breath. It would be so easy to kiss him again but she knew that if she did, it wouldn't stop there. Not with this conflagration that had ignited between them.

A kiss, a good-night kiss, was all it should have been and yet it had escalated into so very much more. She wasn't in a position to let that happen. She didn't dare explore this further, not without some truths between them, and she wasn't ready to tell Judd exactly what she was here for just yet.

The atmosphere between them was filled with possibilities, yet Anna knew she could choose only one. To say goodnight and to let Judd go back to the main house.

"Is this how you say good-night to all your guests?" she asked, in an attempt to lighten the mood that swirled around them.

His lips quirked in a half smile and he lifted his head. "No, only you."

Three words. So simply spoken. The expression in his eyes so honest it went straight to her heart. She clamped down on the feeling, fighting it back so she wouldn't succumb to the lure of the invitation in his gaze. Or to the physical plea that thrummed through every particle of her body.

Her mouth dried. She had no idea of how to respond to him without it sounding careless and glib.

"It's okay, Anna," he said, as if sensing her quandary. "It was only meant to be a simple good-night, nothing more. Unless you want it to be?"

"I...I can't. I—"

"Don't worry," he interrupted. "I'm nothing if not a patient man. And you're worth waiting for. But I promise you this—sooner or later we will make love, and when we do, it will be unforgettable."

His words left her speechless. Unforgettable? Oh, she had no doubt that sex with him would be off the Richter scale. She'd never been into casual encounters, not that anything about Judd Wilson was casual. For him, though, she might have considered it if he hadn't been Charles's son.

Judd pressed his lips against her cheek, almost at the corner of her mouth. All she had to do was turn her head ever so slightly and she could let this lead to its natural and, no doubt, very satisfying conclusion. But she held firm and felt Judd's unspoken acceptance of her refusal.

"I'll pick you up in the morning about nine," he said, letting her go and taking a step away. "Sleep well."

She watched him leave, his long legs eating up the distance along the wide track that led back to the main house. When he was out of sight, she finally let her body sag against the door frame.

Just hours ago, she'd arrived in Australia with one goal in mind—to convince Judd to come with her to New Zealand and reunite with his father. She still wanted—needed—to achieve that goal, but another need was taking over. A need to make the most of her time with Judd, to follow through on the attraction between them and see where it led.

But she knew she couldn't give in. So much rested on how Judd reacted when he learned why she'd come. If things between them got out of hand and he learned the truth too soon, she could inadvertently ruin all of Charles's hopes for reconciliation. She couldn't bear the thought of letting him down like that. Even if it meant closing the door on any chance to explore the sizzling attraction between her and Judd.

Her fingers fluttered to her lips. She could still feel him, still taste him. And God, she still wanted him. How on earth was she going to get through an entire day in his presence without giving in?

Three

The V8 engine of his Aston Martin Vantage roadster purred as Judd drove slowly along the private road that led toward Anna's cottage. A quiet smile of satisfaction played across his face—a total contrast to the frustration that even now held his body deliciously taut with expectation.

He hadn't felt this depth of attraction to a woman in a very long time. Actually, to be completely truthful, he'd never felt quite this level of need in relation to anyone else before.

Today was going to be interesting, very interesting indeed. And tonight? Well, that had the potential to be even better.

The faint burr of his cell phone distracted him. A quick look at the caller ID saw him ease his car to a halt and press a button on his hands-free kit to respond.

"Good morning, Mother. I didn't expect to hear from you this early."

Cynthia didn't waste any time on pleasantries. "I know where she's from."

"Who? Anna?"

"Who else? I was certain she looked familiar, and now I know why. I knew her mother. She worked at Wilson Wines. She was just an office dolly back then—flirted outrageously with the traveling reps. She left when she married one of them, pregnant of course, but I always suspected your father had his eye on her. About three years after we got here I heard that when her husband died, Charles employed her as his *housekeeper*—like anyone expected that was the truth."

Judd tensed. Every time Cynthia mentioned Charles Wilson there was a tone to her voice that set his teeth on edge.

"Did you hear me, Judd?"

"Yes, I heard you. What do you expect me to do about it?"

"Well, confront her, obviously. Her mother was living with Charles, ergo, so was Anna. Find out what she's doing here, because I'd wager she isn't here on holiday. It has to be something to do with your father."

He hated to admit it, but his mother could be right. Ever since they'd met, he'd suspected that Anna was hiding something. And the way she'd looked at him right at their first meeting was as if she was searching his face for a resemblance to someone. Had she been comparing him to his father? He stilled the curl of anger at that thought and at the possibility that his family might be being used by Charles Wilson again. Instead, he channeled his heated emotions into a tool to hone his thinking.

"I'll deal with it. Don't worry."

"I knew she was trouble the second I laid eyes on her," his mother continued. "She's probably working for him, you know. In fact, I wouldn't be surprised, if she's anything like her mother, if she is warming his bed. He always did prefer younger women."

His mother's words were acid in his ears. Cynthia had never let go of the bitterness she felt toward the man she'd left behind in New Zealand. He could still remember the first

day he and Cynthia had arrived at The Masters' and she'd
pointed to the shell of the mansion up on the hill.

Their house in New Zealand had been an identical replica
of the original Masters home—a wedding present built under
Charles's orders for his beautiful bride. Seeing a wrecked,
charred ruin of a house that looked so very much like the
one he'd always known had been a deeply unsettling experience for Judd, especially when Cynthia told him that the ruin
would be a constant reminder of what they'd all lost when
his father had rejected them both and banished them back to
Australia. And it was to be a constant target for all that he
should strive to regain.

His six-year-old mind had been unable to fully understand
what she was saying, hadn't grasped the depth of her obsession with the home she'd lost not once, but twice, and every
day at The Masters' he'd learned what it meant to be rejected
by the man who'd fathered him. Whether it was the pitying
gaze of his uncles and their sometimes overzealous attempts
to be a father figure in his life, or the overheard remarks
made by the staff from time to time when they didn't know
he was listening, he knew exactly what it felt like to be a cast-
off. He snapped his mind back to the present.

"I said I'll deal with it, Mother. By the end of today we'll
know exactly what she's up to."

"Good. I know I can rely on you, Judd. Be careful, my
darling."

Careful? Oh, he'd be more than careful. He disconnected
the call and guided his car once more toward Anna's cottage.
He'd be so careful that Anna Garrick would hardly know
what had hit her.

Anna stood waiting for him on the patio of the cottage.
She looked deceptively fresh and innocent, dressed in layers
of light clothing. He knew she was anything but innocent, especially if her response to him last night had been anything

to go by. He hoped she was up to a little heat, because today promised to be warm in more ways than one.

She walked toward his car as he got out and opened the passenger door for her.

"Nice wheels," she commented.

"I was always a James Bond fanatic as a kid." He smiled. "Some things never get old."

She laughed and settled in the red leather bucket seat, its color a perfect foil for her chestnut-brown hair, he thought as he swung her door closed. As he got back behind the wheel she rummaged in her handbag, pulling out a long bamboo hairpin before twisting her long hair into a knot and securing it at the back of her head.

"I can put the top up if you'd rather," he said, his eyes caught on the elegant line of her neck, the perfection of her jaw.

"No, it's a beautiful day. Let's make the most of it," she answered with a smile that hit him fair and square in the gut and reminded him of just how uncomfortable it had been to walk back to the main house last night.

"Good idea," he agreed and maneuvered the high-performance sports car onto the driveway that led off the property. "You mentioned yesterday that it's your first time in Adelaide," he probed. "What made you decide to come here for a break?"

She remained silent for a moment. From the corner of his eye he could see her press her lips together, as if she was holding back her instinctive answer and taking the time to formulate another.

"It was suggested to me," she said, averting her gaze out the side window.

Oh, he'd put money on the fact it was suggested to her, and by whom. Even without the insight his mother had offered, it was Anna's evasiveness that gave her away. He'd known that she had something to hide, and now that he suspected it involved his father, he was absolutely determined to find out what it was before the day was out. In the meantime, there was nothing, absolutely nothing, stopping him from having a good time along the way.

As they turned out the driveway that led from the vine-yard and out onto the main road heading toward the hills, he saw her gaze pulled up onto the ridge and to the silhouette of the devastated building that stood there. He waited for her to say something, to ask about what had happened. Everyone did, eventually. But she remained silent. The expression on her face was pensive. Some devil of mischief prompted him to comment.

"It was magnificent in its day, you know."

"I beg your pardon?" She turned to face him.

"Masters' Rise, the house up there." He let go of the steering wheel with one hand and gestured up toward the hills.

"It was your family home?"

Did she really not realize, or was she just bluffing? "Not that one, although I lived briefly in a replica of it back in New Zealand when I was young." When she didn't comment on that, he pointed back up the hill. "Masters' Rise was destroyed before my time. My mother and uncles lived there as youngsters, though. I don't think the family pride ever quite recovered from its loss. I know for a fact that my mother's didn't. And it wasn't just losing the house—a good bit of the vineyard was destroyed, as well."

"It wasn't as if they could have done anything to stop it, though, was there?"

"Done anything?"

"Well, it was a bushfire, wasn't it?"

He shot her a piercing glance.

"At least that's what I think I read somewhere," she added hastily.

Oh, good cover, he thought before slowly nodding.

"They were lucky to escape with their lives," he said. "Unfortunately, they didn't have much else—well, not much else but the Masters' tenacity. Rebuilding the house wasn't an option—not when they had to recreate their entire livelihood, as well. It would have taken everything they had left and they were forced to choose between rebuilding their home or re-establishing the vineyards and winery."

"Tough choices. It's a shame they couldn't do both."

"Yeah."

Judd lapsed into silence. Wondering, not for the first time, how different life might have been if the Masters family hadn't been forced into that decision. It couldn't have been easy for his mother and her brothers, starting over from scratch, seeing the life of ease and plenty they'd enjoyed vanishing in a flash. Was that why it had been so easy for Charles Wilson to sweep Cynthia off her feet? Was the life of wealth and luxury he offered truly impossible for a girl, who'd spent so long struggling, to resist?

"So, what's on the agenda for today?" Anna asked, her voice artificially bright. "Last night you mentioned Hahndorf, right? Where and what is it?"

Judd flashed her a smile before transferring his attention back to the road in front of them.

"It was originally a German settlement, established in the early eighteen hundreds. Much of the original architecture still survives and is used today. It's not far from here, but I thought I'd take you a couple of other places first and then we'll head back into Hahndorf for lunch."

"Sounds lovely, thanks. Really, I appreciate you taking time out of your schedule for me."

Judd reached out and caught her hand in his, giving her fingers a gentle squeeze.

"I want to get to know you better, Anna. Can't do that stuck in my office, now, can I?"

To his surprise, a flush of color spread across her cheeks. She blushed? The ingenuousness of the act was totally at odds with the wanton he'd held in his arms last night. Yeah, there was no doubt about it. Anna Garrick intrigued him, and he liked being intrigued—even if it was by someone with a hidden agenda.

Her fingers tingled beneath his touch and Anna felt heat surge through her body, staining her cheeks. God, this effect he had on her would be her undoing. She gently withdrew her hand, distracting herself by poking about in her handbag for a tissue. Her fingertips brushed against the envelope holding the letter from Charles and she pulled her hand out of the bag so rapidly she elicited another one of those piercing looks from Judd.

"So," she said, forcing her heartbeat to resume a more normal rate with a few calming breaths, "where are you taking me first?"

He gestured to the highest peak ahead of them.

"Mount Lofty. From there you'll see the whole of Adelaide spread out before you."

Judd proved himself to be a very efficient tour guide. That he knew the area like the back of his hand was obvious, as was his love and appreciation of his surroundings. By the time they'd taken in the panoramic views of the city and beyond from the peak of Mount Lofty and then strolled through the exquisitely beautiful botanic gardens below, Anna was having a hard time reminding herself that this was no pleasure jaunt.

Judd's fingers were loosely linked in hers as they walked, and every nerve in her body went on high alert, focusing intently on the scant physical connection they shared. Wishing against everything that the connection could be deepened and intensified.

She fought to regain control of her senses. She'd be crazy to embark on anything physical with Judd Wilson. Totally and utterly crazy. But no matter what her head told her, her body demanded something else entirely.

In her bag, she felt her cell phone discreetly vibrate. The only person who would be calling her would be Charles. Her stomach lurched. Was he okay? He hadn't looked well when she'd left Auckland yesterday. Extracting her fingers from Judd's light clasp, she reached into her bag.

"Excuse me, I need to take this," she said, putting the phone to her ear and turning to walk a few steps away from him.

"Have you met him yet?" Charles's voice sounded strong and healthy.

"Yes, I have," she said guardedly, wishing she'd let the call go to her message service and then phoned Charles back when she had a little more privacy.

"Well, what's he like? Have you given him the letter yet? What did he say?"

Charles's questions fired at her with the less-than-subtle force of a battering ram and she created a little more distance between herself and the subject of those questions.

"It's hard to say at the moment. No, and nothing yet," she answered each question in turn.

"You're with him now, aren't you?"

"Yes," she replied. "Look, it's really not a good time to talk. Can I get back to you later?"

Please say "yes," she silently begged. In response, Charles's hearty chuckle filled her ear.

"Not a good time, eh? Okay, then, I'll leave you to it. But make sure you call me back later today."

"Yes, certainly. I'll do that. Goodbye."

"Anna, don't hang up!"

She sighed. "Yes?"

"I'm counting on you. I *need* my son with me."

"I'll do my best."

"Thank you, darling girl."

He disconnected the call and Anna felt her shoulders sag with the reminder of what he expected of her.

"Bad news?" Judd asked.

"No, not really," Anna hedged.

"Anything I can help with?"

She fought back the strangled laugh that rose in her throat. If only he knew. But no, the last thing she could do was divulge the details of that phone call. Not yet, anyway. She shook her head and pushed her phone back in her bag.

"It was just work, I can deal with it later. I'm starving," she said, trying to shift the conversation onto safer ground. "How about that lunch you promised me?"

"Your wish is my command," Judd said, taking her hand again and lifting it to his lips.

His blue eyes gleamed, letting Anna know in no uncertain terms that he was definitely open to more than just lunch. Again that surge of heat swirled deep inside her, making her body tighten in anticipation. She fought to paint a smile on her lips. This was all going to be so much harder than she had ever imagined.

On the short drive to Hahndorf, Charles's words kept echoing around in her head, *I need my son with me.* An unexpected flash of anger rose within her. Charles was so bent on reuniting with his long-lost son that he'd completely forgotten he had a daughter right by his side. A daughter who understood his wine importation and distribution business better, almost, than her own father. A daughter who'd spent her whole life stepping up in an attempt to fill the near insurmountable gap left when Cynthia had taken Judd to Australia.

Anna wondered again about the contents of the letter that weighed so heavily in her handbag. She knew Charles was planning on offering Judd an incentive to return, but he hadn't shared the details with her. Whatever carrot he'd chosen to dangle, what would it mean to the sister who didn't even remember Judd? The one who worked so hard to please her father, for no reward other than his love and hard-won approval? Anna adored Charles with every breath in her body. He'd been the only father figure she'd ever known, but she worried that he'd overstepped the mark with this obsession with Judd and that he'd damage his relationship with Nicole irrevocably.

"What sort of work do you do that they need to call you when you're on vacation?"

Judd's voice interrupted her thoughts and made her start. She'd been dreading this question and had already decided that a vague response would be her best bet.

"Oh, I'm a P.A."

"You must be pretty important to your boss if he can't keep from calling you."

Anna forced her features to relax into a smile. "I've worked for him since I left school. We're probably closer than most boss/employee relationships."

She caught Judd's piercing look before his eyes resumed their surveillance of the road in front of them. He began to slow the car as they approached a township, and Anna let out an involuntary exclamation of delight as they entered the main road. Lined with massive trees and with quaint tin-roofed buildings, she'd have thought she'd stepped back in time if it hadn't been for the bustle of people and modern vehicles that lined the street.

Judd expertly backed the Aston Martin into a car space and came around to open Anna's door.

"I'm surprised he let you out of his sight, if you're so *close*," he said, his words weighted with something that Anna couldn't quite put her finger on.

"I'm my own woman," she answered.

"I'm pleased to hear it," Judd said in return, taking her hand and tucking it firmly in the crook of his elbow. "Because I don't like to share."

"I've heard that trait was reserved for only children," Anna said with a soft laugh, trying to defuse the heady rush of excitement his words stimulated inside her.

"What makes you think I'm not an only child?"

Oh, Lord, she'd nearly stepped right in it. She scoured her memory quickly, although deep down she knew that no one here in Adelaide had mentioned his estranged family to her.

"Oh, I don't know. I just assumed, since you grew up here surrounded by your cousins, that sharing was a natural part of your life."

She held her breath, hoping he'd be satisfied with her reply. To her surprise, he let out a short laugh.

"Yeah, I suppose that'd be a natural assumption."

"So, are you?" she probed, wanting some insight into how he might feel about the sister he hadn't seen in years.

"An only child?" He shrugged. "It's complicated. My parents divorced when I was young, and they split my sister and me up at the same time. I was six, she was just one year old."

"Isn't that unusual? That your father kept your sister?"

"He didn't want me—my mother did."

Judd's words, so simply spoken, hinted strongly at the hurt that had to lie behind them. Anna wanted to protest. To tell him that his father wanted him very much indeed, but they weren't her words to say.

"Have you ever wanted to see your sister? Get to know her?" she pressed, taking a different tack.

"Why the sudden interest?"

"Oh, nothing. It's just that, as I told you last night, I *am* an only child and I always wanted siblings."

"The human condition, huh? Always wanting what we can't have."

"I suppose so," Anna admitted, sorry that he'd so deftly avoided answering her question.

They walked along the shady sidewalk, stopping every now and then to wander into one of the many galleries before they crossed the road to take an umbrella-covered table outside an obviously very popular inn. Anna pulled the pin from her hair and shook it loose from its temporary restraint. She didn't miss the glow of pure male appreciation in Judd's eyes as she did so and felt her body warm in response.

"Would you like a menu, or would you like me to choose for you?" Judd asked.

"Go ahead and order for me. I eat just about everything."

"What would you like to drink? A glass of wine?"

Anna eyed a nearby patron swigging at a foam-topped beer. "One of those," she said, pointing.

"Beer?"

"Sure. Don't tell me you're one of those people who don't think women should drink beer."

"Not at all." He laughed. "In fact, I plan to join you."

When the waitress came over he ordered their meals and two beers. They didn't have to wait long before the food and drinks arrived. Anna gasped when she saw the size of the platter placed before them.

"It's their Taste of Germany. You couldn't come here without trying it," Judd said.

"I'll take your word for it. I sure hope *you're* hungry, too," Anna replied, taking a sip of her chilled beer. "Mmm, that's good."

She grew so engrossed in the meal and their surroundings that she didn't notice when a family with several children raced by their table. One of the kids lost his balance when his foot hooked into the handle of her bag, which she'd placed on the ground by the table leg. Anna's hands flew to stabilize the beer mugs on the table as it rocked under the impact of the youngster's clumsiness.

"Oh, no! I'm so sorry," his harried mother said, rushing to pick up the belongings that had scattered from Anna's bag.

"Don't worry, it's okay," Anna assured her, reaching for the items the woman had so far gathered and shoving them back in her bag. "Really, it's my fault. I shouldn't have left the strap hanging out like that."

Judd had risen from his chair and was helping to collect Anna's things. Too late she saw the stark-white envelope that had been ejected from its hiding place. His long-fingered hand hovered over it and her heart sank to the soles of her feet as she registered the exact moment he identified the name on the front.

He settled back in his chair, handing most of her things back to her, but holding the envelope between his fingers as if it contained something dangerous inside. The mother and her son moved on, rejoining the rest of their family, but Anna didn't even notice. All she could do was stare at Judd and the flat packet in his hands.

"Care to explain this?" he said, his voice suddenly devoid of the warmth it had contained only moments ago.

Anna took a deep breath. "It's a letter."

"I can see that. It looks like a letter to *me*."

She couldn't maintain eye contact and instead dropped her gaze to her lap, where her fingers knotted in anxiety. This was all wrong. She'd wanted to give him the letter when she was ready, when she was in control and when she could better gauge what his reaction would be. Not in a public place like this, with no warning and no chance to prepare him for the letter's contents.

"It is," she said softly.

She flinched as she heard the envelope tear open. Her stomach tied in a knot of unbelievable proportions as the sound of a single sheet of paper being unfolded overwhelmed the noise of the diners and sightseers around them.

Anna finally lifted her gaze and watched as Judd read the letter his father had written. The letter that had the capacity to change all their lives. When he'd finished, he neatly re-folded the sheet and put it back in the envelope. Still he said nothing. A shiver of fear danced down her spine. He was calm, too calm. She'd seen Charles get like this and she knew that it was only the quiet before the storm. What was coming could only be cataclysmic.

She reached across the table, touching his forearm. He shook off her touch as if she were nothing more than an annoying insect.

"Judd—" she started, but whatever she'd been about to say died in her throat when he met her eyes and she felt the full fury of the glacial fire reflected there.

"Who the hell are you and why are you really here?"

Four

Across the table Anna stared at him in shock. She felt all color drain from her face and a numb coldness settle in the pit of her stomach. She'd done this all wrong. She should have just followed Charles's orders right from the start to make an appointment to see Judd and tell him from the outset why she was there. She took a deep breath before speaking.

"I…I've told you who I am. I'm Anna Garrick. And…" Her mouth dried, forcing her to pause for a moment, and swallow, before continuing, "And I'm here because your father desperately wants to make amends for the past."

"If he's so keen to make amends, why isn't he here himself?" Judd demanded.

His skin had gone taut across his features, lending an implacable hardness to his face, and his eyes burned with a hard blue intensity.

"He didn't tell you in the letter?"

"I want to hear it from you. Why did he not come here himself? Was he too ashamed to face up to me, to face up to the truth that his own pride and his stupid accusations are responsible for having torn our family apart in the first place?"

Anna made a small noise of protest. It wasn't like that. Sure, she'd heard that Charles hadn't been an angel at the time his marriage to Cynthia had fallen irrevocably apart—who ever was when under extreme pressure?—but from what her mother had told her, she knew that Cynthia had done plenty of damage, as well. Charles definitely hadn't been solely responsible for what had happened, no matter what Judd's mother might have told him.

"Well?" Judd demanded.

"He's unwell. His doctor wouldn't clear him to travel." The diabetes that had plagued Charles for so many years had worsened, in part due to his late diagnosis and subsequent reluctance to follow medical recommendations to prevent further damage to his body. His kidneys were showing signs that renal failure could be just around the corner.

"How convenient."

Judd lifted his stein and took a healthy swig of its contents, and Anna felt the initial stirrings of her own anger rise in response to his derision.

"It isn't convenient at all, actually. Look, I'm not privy to exactly what he said in his letter to you, but I have a pretty good idea of what he's asking. He wants to see you again. To get to know you before he—" Suddenly overwhelmed with emotion, her voice broke.

"Before he what?"

"Before he dies," she said shakily.

"You care about him?" Judd's voice was devoid of emotion.

"More than you could ever understand," she said, forcing herself to pull it together. "He is not a well man, Judd. Please, this could be your last chance to get to know him. He's your father, surely you owe him that."

"Owe him?" He snorted a laugh. "That's rich. I don't owe

him anything and I haven't exactly missed out on having him in my life. I don't see why that should change, although he has certainly attempted to sweeten the pot to entice me back to New Zealand."

"Sweeten the pot?" She felt a building sense of dread. Just what kind of incentive had Charles offered?

"You really don't know?"

"If I knew, would I be asking?" she snapped.

"Strange, given that you're his valued *employee,* and given—by your own admission—how *close* you are and how much you care about him, that he didn't see the need to apprise you of his intentions."

She didn't like his unspoken insinuation that there was something unsavory between her and Charles. Sure, she loved him—like a father. But how could she explain that to Judd now? He'd never believe her.

Judd leaned back in his chair and fixed her with his intense gaze. "It seems that your esteemed employer wishes to offer me a controlling interest in the family business."

"He what?"

A controlling interest? Just like that? Black spots swam before Anna's eyes and she gulped at the air. How could Charles do that to Nicole? How could *she* have done that to Nicole? Anna knew her best friend had standards just as high as Charles's when it came to loyalty and honesty. When she found out that Anna had been the messenger who had gone behind Nicole's back to practically hand deliver Charles's company to Judd, would Nicole ever forgive her?

"And that's not all. Apparently, he wants to assign the family home to me, as well." He casually waved the letter in the air. "All to do with whatever I please."

Anna couldn't believe her ears. "He wouldn't do something like that. You have no loyalty to Charles, no loyalty to Wilson Wines. For all we know, you'd just sell off your share to someone who didn't give a damn. Charles would never do something so rash."

Would he? Had he become so desperate to mend the vast chasm between father and son that he was prepared to offer the world on a platter? This would destroy Nicole. She'd grown up in the New Zealand house—it was still her home. And she'd poured her heart and soul into the business—surely not to simply see half of it handed over to her brother? Charles couldn't be so cruel.

But Anna knew full well that Charles was capable of doing such a thing. Single-minded to a fault, his aim was to return his son to his side before he died. When his doctors had confirmed that time might be running out, he'd gone after his goal to bring Judd back into his life with every weapon at his disposal. He'd do whatever it took, even if it meant hurting the daughter who loved him so very much.

Ever since the posthumous delivery of a letter from his former partner and biggest business rival, Thomas Jackson, he'd become obsessed with Judd, with somehow rebuilding a bond between them. Anna hadn't been privy to the contents of the letter but she'd wager her very generous salary that it had to do with the rift between the business partners and Cynthia and Judd leaving New Zealand very shortly after. She'd often wondered if Thomas Jackson and Cynthia had been lovers.

Which begged the question—had Charles believed Judd was not his son?

Judd passed the letter across to her.

"Read it for yourself."

The words blurred before her eyes and she blinked to clear them. It was true. There, in Charles's scrawling black handwriting, was his desperate appeal to the son he'd turned his back on twenty-five years ago. She knew what it must have cost the older man to put his emotions in words like this. Never a demonstrative man, it shocked her to see him pour his heart out onto the page. Ever hedging his bets, though, he'd insisted on Judd undergoing DNA testing to prove he was, without a shadow of a doubt, Charles's child. Ah, so there had been some doubt. Now everything began to make sense.

She finished scanning the letter and neatly folded it before handing it back to Judd.

"I had no idea he had planned this. Will you accept his offer?" she asked.

"He insults my mother, even after all this time, and you think I'm going to leap at his offer?"

"Insults Cynthia?" She didn't follow his reasoning.

"The DNA test. He wants proof she didn't cheat on him when I was conceived. It's obvious, no matter what he says in that letter, he hasn't changed a bit. He still expects to call all the shots. And then there's you."

"Me?"

"What's your role in all this? Did he expect you to also sweeten the deal?"

Anna felt a flush rise in her cheeks. "I don't think I like what you're suggesting."

"Well, you can't blame me. You come to my family's home, you fail to identify yourself or your reasons for being here and you show yourself to be very receptive to attention from me. You certainly didn't object last night when I kissed you."

"That was…"

Words failed her.

"It was what, Anna? Going over and above the call of duty?"

Anna bit back the retort that sprang so readily to her lips and forced herself to calm down.

"I did what I came to do, you have the letter, you've read it. Now the ball is in your court."

And she'd failed Charles, she admitted to herself. The

knowledge lodged like a heavy ball of painful regret knotted tight within her chest. The most important thing he'd ever asked of her and she'd screwed it up.

"Please, I beg of you, don't let what I've done influence your decision in any way. Charles wanted me to be upfront with you. It was my choice to hold back my real reasons for being here."

"Why?"

"I knew he wanted to extend an olive branch, but I was concerned about how you might feel about him and whether you would take advantage of him. He's an old man, old before his time because of his illness. He doesn't deserve any more misery in his life."

"And that's your considered opinion?"

"Of course it is. Look, you don't know him. You probably barely remember him. Whatever happened in the past is past. It can't be undone. Can't you put it aside and consider what it would mean to him to make amends with you now?"

Judd stared at her for a moment, his expression not giving any sign of what he might be thinking. The knot of dread tightened even further.

Put the past behind him? Did she have even the faintest idea what she was asking? Of course she didn't. She hadn't been torn from the father who had adored him one minute and then refused to look at him the next. She hadn't been transplanted into another family, another world, and been told to "man up" because his mother expected him to be strong. He'd lost count of the number of times he'd watched cars arrive at The Masters' and hoped against hope that his father would alight from one of them. That he'd come to say it had all been a mistake.

But what his six-year-old heart had wished for had never happened and, in time, he'd learned not to scan the parents' faces at school events for the man whose features he'd always been told were an older version of his own. He'd learned to inure himself from the hope that one day his life would return to what it had been before.

And it had made him a stronger man. A man who knew that the only person he could, or should, rely upon was himself.

His first instinct on reading his father's entreaty was to ball it up and to tell Anna to take it back to Charles-bloody-Wilson and to tell the old man to put it where the sun doesn't shine. But then rationality overrode the deviation into emotionalism.

Without realizing it, his long-estranged father had actually given Judd the opportunity he'd quietly dreamed of for many a year—payback. Not only for rejecting the son who'd so earnestly idolized him, but for what he'd done to Cynthia.

Judd had heard the story from his mother more times than he could count—after pulling her away from her home and her family, Charles had neglected her. Ignored her. Prioritized every concern over and above his relationship with his wife. And when Cynthia, in her loneliness and frustration, had started spending more time away from home, trying to find friends and activities to fill the void left by her husband's absence, Charles had turned into a possessive monster, constantly jealous and utterly convinced she was cheating on him.

It had all culminated in the fight that had led Charles to kick Judd and his mother out of the house. And that was the last Judd had seen of his father. There had been no phone calls. No letters. No visits. Charles had clearly washed his hands of both of them for the past twenty-five years.

And now, this was Judd's chance to pay him back in kind for all the pain he and his mother had suffered. With the controlling interest in the company, Charles was placing the weapons right into his hands. Everything his mother had told him about the past had shown Charles up for a man who'd always put his business before his family. Judd knew exactly where to strike to cause the most pain, to exact the deepest satisfaction.

He needed time to think, to consolidate the plans burgeoning in his mind, but he had no doubt that he'd shortly be accepting his father's offer. No doubt at all.

He looked over at Anna—his eyes raking over her and taking in the lustrous length of her hair, her exquisite beauty, her enticing feminine curves. She was all woman from the top of her head to the tips of her toes. Even now, as angry as he was, she still had the capacity to excite him, to incite within him the desire to possess her in every manner of the word.

A tug of regret pulled deep inside. His mother's warning had done little to dim his attraction to Anna, but the letter had cast a whole new light on things. Maybe her reluctance to deliver it to him had its basis in something other than what she'd admitted. Maybe she was worried about what his entry back into his father's life would do to affect her position there and what she stood to gain from Charles Wilson after his death. Charles had chosen her as his ambassador in his attempt at reunion, so he obviously trusted her implicitly. By her own admission she said she and the old man were close—that she cared for him *deeply*. How close, exactly? Were they lovers, as his mother suspected? If that was true, it would no doubt give him a double-edged sense of satisfaction when he eventually seduced her.

But as with everything else, it would wait until the time was perfectly right. For now, he wanted her away from The Masters' and somewhere else, where she could do no harm.

He gestured to the food before them.

"Are you going to eat that?"

She shook her head. "I couldn't, not now."

"Let's go, then."

"Back to the vineyard?"

"To get your things, yes, and then to take you into the city."

"The city?"

"To a hotel. It may surprise you, but funnily enough, I don't want you around my family right now. My mother's been through quite enough over the years without adding the insult of your presence."

She flinched beneath his words, her face paling even more.

"Fine," she replied tightly. "When will you let me know your decision about Charles?"

"In good time. You aren't due to return to Auckland for another few days, is that correct?"

"Yes, on Friday morning."

"I'll let you know by then."

Anna paced the terrace of her hotel room, her cell phone to her ear.

"I'm sorry, Charles. I screwed up. I should have just done what you told me to do."

Charles was surprisingly philosophical.

"What's done is done. It's certainly no worse or better than what's gone on before this. Let's just hope he comes to his senses and comes home before it's too late."

Before it's too late. Her heart squeezed. It wasn't like Charles to be melodramatic. She knew he was deteriorating, but had he kept something from her? Was his health worse than even she suspected?

"I still can't believe you're prepared to go to those lengths to bring him home."

"It's his birthright, Anna. You know that as much as I do."

"But what about Nicole? Have you talked to her about this yet?"

"I wasn't going to say anything to her until he's back and we know for certain he's mine. Until then, it's a moot point.

And you're not to say a word, either. You promised me, Anna."

She sighed. "Yes, I know. I won't say a word, but keeping the truth away from her is only going to hurt all of us."

"Let me be the judge of that."

"And the house, Charles. Why the house, too? You're talking about taking Nicole's home right out from under her feet."

"Yours, too," he reminded her with a surprisingly curt note in his voice. "But I will have to trust him to do the right thing and to continue to provide the two of you with a roof over your heads. If I don't do that, if I don't prove to him that I'm prepared to accept him fully, it will never work. Besides, he grew up with the Masters—I know how they feel about the house. Judd is already running their company, so offering him mine might not be enough of a draw. But no one else can give him that house."

"What makes you so sure you have to take such drastic steps?"

"Because that's what it would take to lure me back if someone had done the same thing to me."

If Nicole ever spoke to her again after this it would be a miracle. Anna felt a chill run the length of her spine. She stepped inside her hotel room and slid the glass door closed, but even so, she continued to feel cold. What Charles was doing was wrong, she knew it to the soles of her feet. But it was too late now. The offer had been made. She could only hope against hope that Judd would be man enough to turn it down. That he'd accept his father for who he was without the added enticement of half of Wilson Wines and the home that Charles had built for Cynthia all those years ago.

"So you're not going to give her any prior warning. You're just going to present her with a brother and say this is how it's going to be from now on?"

"They are my children, it's my company and my home, so this is my decision. Don't overstep your boundaries, Anna."

His words stung.

"Of course," she said in reply, even as other more impassioned words filled her mind.

"He said he'll give you his decision by Friday?"

"Yes, he did."

"Let's hope it's the right one. Let me know as soon as you've spoken to him."

"I will."

"Good. I'll look forward to it."

His business done, the call was over, leaving Anna alone to stare at the darkening hills in the distance and to wonder just how all of this was going to end.

Five

"I told you I was right." Cynthia's eyes gleamed triumphantly.

Judd merely nodded. He'd spent the latter part of the afternoon locked in his office, looking at his schedule and seeing where, and to whom, he could apportion his workload. It was one advantage of having several cousins all working within the same family business, he conceded. There were plenty of people just as invested as he was in making sure The Masters' continued to run smoothly. Between his cousins and the well-trained staff they also employed, Judd felt confident he could leave the company in good hands.

Once he had everything worked out to his satisfaction, he asked his mother for a private meeting. Her delight at the enticement Charles was offering was palpable. He hadn't seen her this animated, ever.

"When will you let them know your decision?" his mother pressed.

"On Friday morning. I'll be too busy tomorrow bringing

everyone up to speed with their additional duties to be talking to Anna Garrick."

As soon as he said her name he felt the now-familiar tug of desire. He'd made some inquiries. She lived with Charles Wilson, which confirmed she was indeed far, far more than simply his father's P.A. Stealing her away from him, right under the old man's roof, was undeniably appealing but something he'd have to approach very carefully.

"Do you know how long the DNA testing will take?"

"I believe establishing paternity is a relatively simple process. A few days to a week for the results."

"You know, I cannot believe he would stoop to that. He only needs to look at you to know I never betrayed him."

She injected a note of pathos in her voice, but Judd had heard it all before. When she didn't elicit the response from her son that she obviously wanted, she continued.

"We'll finally have back what should have been ours all along," she said, her voice now stronger, showing her true mettle.

"The house?"

He should have known that would be the most important thing to her. He had to admit to a certain curiosity himself to go back to the place that had been his home for the first six years of his life. But where his mother seemed to want to reclaim the building, Judd was far more inclined to go after it with a wrecking ball...just as he planned to do with Wilson Wines. He'd take his father's legacy apart bit by bit, and when he was done, he'd be back here at The Masters', picking up the reins of his job once again. At that point, his mother could have the darn house for all he cared.

"I'll have to redecorate it, you know. Restore it to its former glory."

"How do you know it's not perfect just the way it is?"

She rolled her eyes at him. "Judd, darling, it's been twenty-five years since I've set foot in there. There will be work to do, I'm sure. I poured my heart into that house—no one loved it more than I did."

"Let's not put the cart before the horse, hmm?"

"Of course. We have to satisfy your father's ridiculous demands first. How long do you think you'll be away?"

"I don't see this taking more than a month."

"That long?"

He thought of his plans for the delectable Miss Garrick. A month? Maybe longer would be better. He wanted to savor this victory.

"Maybe longer. We'll see how it pans out."

After his mother left his office, he sat back in his leather chair and stared out the window at the vineyard and winery that occupied his immediate view. He enjoyed his work here, there was no doubt about that, and he was good at it. But he had become bored in recent months, feeling stifled by the lack of opportunity to make changes. Now, perhaps, even if only for a short time, he'd have the chance to really stretch his mind as he implemented his plans. Plans to dismantle his father's empire and steal his mistress right out from under his nose.

Anna woke on Friday morning in a state of nerves and automatically reached for her cell phone, as she had several times throughout last night. Still nothing from Judd Wilson. Just how fine was he going to cut this? She looked at the time on her phone and raced for the bathroom—the broken night's rest having made her sleep past the time she'd wanted to rise. A car was coming to pick her up and take her to the airport for her flight in about half an hour. She'd already packed her things the night before. All she needed to do was shower and dress in the clothes she'd left out for the journey home.

She was down in the lobby of the hotel and signing off her hotel account when a trickle of awareness filtered through the parting words of the hotel receptionist. He was here. Did that mean she'd succeeded? Was he accompanying her back to New Zealand, or maybe he was merely here to tell her in person that her quest on Charles's behalf had failed.

She knew she had to turn around. Had to face him. It took every ounce of strength in her body to paste a smile on her face and turn away from the reception desk. The moment her eyes lighted upon him she felt the excruciating pull of attraction. How could she still be so drawn to him when he'd been so awful to her? She'd asked herself that question over and over the past two nights, especially each time she'd woken from yet another tormented dream explicitly featuring the man standing directly opposite her.

He'd be a formidable poker player, she thought irrationally. He let nothing show in his expression as to what he was thinking, or whatever decision he'd reached.

"Are you ready?" he said coolly.

"What? No good morning?" she said, unable to keep the acerbity from her voice.

He merely raised one dark brow. Anna grabbed the handle of her wheeled suitcase and headed for the front door.

"Let me take that for you," Judd said, blocking her way and collapsing the extended handle and swinging the case up in one hand.

She'd packed for only three and a half days, and she hadn't packed light, yet he carried the bag as if it weighed nothing. Realizing he was headed for the automatic opening doors and to the dark limousine outside, she propelled herself after him.

"Wait, I've ordered a taxi."

"And I've canceled it. We'll travel together to the airport."

"And then?" she asked, suddenly tired of the game.

Was he coming back to Auckland with her or not? The not knowing was playing havoc with her stomach.

"And then we'll check in to our flight."

"So you're accepting Charles's offer?"

He handed her case to the waiting driver and then opened

the rear door, gesturing for her to be seated inside the dark, leather-filled interior. She halted at the door, not wanting to get inside until she knew exactly where things stood.

"I've consented to undergoing the tests and when my father is satisfied, yes, I will be accepting his offer."

Anna didn't know whether to feel elated or devastated. A hollow emptiness filled her heart. Unable to speak, she nodded in acknowledgment of his words and settled herself in the car. She was grateful when Judd took the passenger seat in the front of the vehicle. She needed some time to gather her thoughts, to prepare herself for what was to come.

The journey to the airport was short, and before she alighted she asked for a moment to call Charles.

"That won't be necessary," Judd said smoothly, offering her his hand to help her from the car.

"Why not?" she asked, reluctantly putting her hand in his and bracing herself for the jolt of electricity she knew would come next.

Sure enough, the merest touch of his fingers was enough to set her heart beating faster. Arousal flared deep inside. Not the type she was used to—the slow, gentle warming of mutual attraction. No, this was far more primal than that. Sharper, more instinctive, and it made her body ache in response. She pulled her hand from his, but the sensation still lingered.

"Because I've already spoken with him."

"You spoke with him?" Anna fought to keep the incredulity from her voice.

"Is that so strange?"

"Well, yes. Especially considering your reaction to his letter."

"As you said on Wednesday, the past *is* past."

She looked at him in disbelief, hardly daring to believe that he actually meant it. A man like Judd Wilson was too intense, too driven to simply put the past in a time capsule and lock it away. He had to have an ulterior motive.

"What? No comment?" Judd gently goaded.

"How was he?"

"He sounded fine. Surprised to hear from me, but I'd say he's cautiously optimistic."

So this thing would play out after all, Anna thought as the driver hefted their cases from the trunk of the car and went to procure a luggage cart. Not waiting for the man to return, she pulled the handle up on her case and headed for the departure check-in area, but within seconds Judd walked at her side, pushing his own much larger cases on the cart in front of him. Basically, everything was out of her hands from here on in. She could only hope that Nicole would forgive her for her part in the machinations of her father. But somehow Anna doubted any of what was to come would be that easy.

Charles's driver and handyman, Patrick Evans, collected them from Auckland International Airport. They were nearly home. Evans drove slowly and inexorably toward the massive gothic mansion Charles had built from the original plans of Masters' Rise—the headlights of the car sweeping the camellia-lined driveway in Auckland's premier suburb of Remuera. Anna had to admit she was relieved to see the house.

Back in Australia, it had shocked her to see the ruins on the hill overlooking the vineyard. Suddenly the home that had always provided her with security didn't seem so permanent after all. Of course, bushfires were nonexistent in the city, virtually nonexistent in New Zealand, really, and nowadays Charles had a state-of-the-art fire detection and sprinkler system throughout the house. But there were plenty of things other than bushfires that could tear a house—and a family—apart.

With the time distance between Adelaide and Auckland, and the flight time in between, it was already dark as they pulled up in front of the house, but clever external lighting showed the property off to its glorious advantage. Anna observed Judd, sitting opposite her in the limousine, and watched his reaction.

"So that's what it looked like," he said solemnly, his eyes raking the two-storied, pinkish-red brick building. "My memories from before we left were...incomplete."

"Apparently it's very true to the original, with extensive modernization, of course. Despite its size, it's still very much a home."

The car rolled to a stop outside the front portico, prominently marked by an ivy-covered, three-storied turret complete with a green-aged copper cupola.

"It's your home."

He made it a statement, rather than a question. A statement she chose to ignore as she stepped from the car and assisted Patrick in removing the luggage from the spacious trunk of the limousine.

The front doors opened and Anna turned, expecting to see Charles, but instead it was Nicole who stood there. Elegant and tall in her well-cut black suit and with her long dark hair pulled back into a ponytail that exposed her pale face, Nicole stared at the man who was her brother.

"I didn't believe him when he told me you were coming," she said, her voice flat—devoid of emotion.

Instantly Anna's defensive instincts went on full alert. Nicole was usually very outgoing, impulsive and generous to a fault. This frozen pale facsimile of her best friend was something she'd never seen before.

Nicole came down the steps and halted near Anna.

"Why didn't you tell me?"

Even as Anna flinched at the question, she found herself internally debating what Nicole was really asking. There was no way to know how much Charles had told her. Had he only announced that Judd was coming back to them—or had he explained all the rest of it, too, all the things Charles had promised to bring his son home?

Either way, her answer was the same. "He asked me not to."

"And your loyalty to him is greater than to me?" Nicole said softly, the hurt in her words flaying Anna like cold winter rain.

"That's not fair, Nicole."

"No, you're right. But there's a lot that's not fair about all this, isn't there?"

Pain reflected in her friend's large brown eyes. Anna put a hand on Nicole's arm and squeezed gently.

"You know I would have spoken to you if I could."

Nicole nodded and turned back to Judd, who'd remained silent as a statue.

"So, brother, I suppose I should welcome you home."

She held out her arms and to Anna's surprise he stepped into her embrace, holding her gently before releasing her and stepping back.

Judd was shocked at the depth of emotion he felt when he saw his sister at the top of the stairs to the house. She'd been a year old when he'd left, and in his mind he'd never imagined her fully grown. Another mark against his father, he thought savagely. All those years wasted.

"We have some catching up to do," he said.

To his surprise, Nicole laughed. "Well, if that's not the understatement of the century. Come inside. Dad's waiting for you."

Judd turned to Anna, who'd watched his reunion with his sister with a solemn expression on her face. "Are you coming?"

"I think this should be just for the three of you. I'll catch up with you all at dinner."

Nicole made a sound of protest. "Don't be silly, Anna. You know Dad will expect you there, too."

Anna looked at him, as if waiting for his approval.

"Sure," he said.

If the stiltedness between her and his sister was any indication, perhaps Nicole didn't entirely approve of Anna and their father's closeness.

Nicole hooked her arm in his. In her three-inch heels they were almost of a height and together they walked up the stairs and into the house that was shortly to become all his. One thing was clear to Judd—Charles hadn't gotten any better about showing consideration to the women in his life. It was obvious Nicole wasn't aware of the full extent of Charles's plans for him. He doubted she'd be this friendly if she knew. That would have to be a bridge to cross at a later date. First, he had to go face-to-face with the man who'd cast him from his home and his country twenty-five years ago, and he had to do it with a civil tongue in his head.

Judd's memories of his father had been of a vital man who exuded energy and bonhomie the moment he stepped in a room. The man who shakily rose to his feet as they entered a large salon was a mere shadow of whom he'd been. Despite Charles's unmistakable frailty, Judd's long-harbored anger at his father's abandonment did not lessen.

"Here he is, Dad," Nicole said.

"Judd—"

"Sir," Judd said, stepping forward and offering his hand.

He watched his father, searching for the man he remembered but seeing little of the vibrancy of his memories. Charles's hair was now steel-gray instead of the black Judd remembered, and his posture was less erect, his figure more portly than fit. But even though his father was obviously unwell, there was a keen intelligence that still gleamed in his eyes as they stood face-to-face. Those blue eyes, very like his own, scoured his features as silence stretched out between them. Something in his appearance must have satisfied the older man, because he gave a short nod and gestured to Judd to sit down.

Anna crossed the room and took the seat on the sofa next to Charles, her hand on his forearm as she leaned closer to whisper something in his ear. A fierce wave of something not unlike jealousy rose from deep inside Judd. Her body language shouted a familiarity between Anna and Charles that screamed loud and clear. A familiarity that Judd silently promised would soon change.

"Don't fuss, Anna. I'm fine," Charles protested, taking her hand and holding it in his for a moment before releasing it. "Now, let's not beat around the bush. You know I want proof you're my son."

Judd felt his hackles rise. "I know I'm your son. I couldn't be anyone else's."

"I'm sure that's what your mother told you," Charles commented, "but you must understand I need to be one hundred percent certain."

"I told you I'm prepared to be tested," Judd said, holding on to his temper by the merest edge.

His mother was no angel, but he knew she told the truth when she said he was Charles Wilson's son. She wouldn't lie about something as vital as that. Not to him.

"Good, good. We can attend to that on Monday and courier the samples to the lab here in Auckland. They offer an express service and promise paternity results within forty-eight hours. It's a shame Anna didn't get you back earlier and that we have to wait out the weekend before we can complete the tests."

He couldn't help it. He had to ask. "Why the sudden urgency? You've waited twenty-five years, surely another two days won't be a problem."

Charles shot him a glance and then smiled proudly. "Well, you certainly sound like me. Straight to the point, hmm?"

"I find it doesn't pay to beat around the bush in important matters."

"No, it never does."

Judd merely looked at him, waiting for him to stop hedging and get to the point. The air in the room became uncomfortable, and in his periphery Judd saw Nicole glance from him to their father.

"I'd like to know, too," she blurted, a tremor in her voice. "Why now, Dad?"

Charles looked at his daughter, a frown of censure on his forehead. "Don't go getting all emotional, Nicole. It's no secret that I'm not getting any younger or any healthier. It's time for me to get everything in order."

"Why did you drag Anna into this? Why send her to do your dirty work?" Nicole persisted.

"That's enough, young lady. I'm still the head of this household and I'm still the head of Wilson Wines. Don't question me."

Nicole slumped in her chair, all the fight gone out of her in a flash. Judd felt a momentary pang of regret for what she must be going through. He'd make it up to her somehow, he promised silently. She deserved something for having put up with the old man all these years without anyone to stand up for her. It was something he'd have done, if given half a chance.

A movement at the door caught everyone's attention.

"Excuse me, sir, but dinner is served in the dining room," a uniformed middle-aged woman said.

"Thank you, Mrs. Evans," Charles said, dismissing the housekeeper and turning back to Judd. "We keep regular hours here for mealtimes—my diabetes, you know."

Charles rose to his feet, refusing Anna's offer of assistance, and led the way through to the dining room. Each room Judd set foot in gave him a weird sense of déjà vu. Although his memories of living here were faded and sketchy, the old photos of Masters' Rise that had been passed on by friends after the fire were imprinted in his mind. This house truly was a complete replica of his mother's old home. No wonder she was so bitter about being made to leave.

He made a silent promise—Cynthia would return to triumph over all this again.

They'd been back one day short of a week. Anna sat at her desk, finding it nearly impossible to concentrate on the work ahead of her. Judd had traveled into the office with Charles this morning, and the two of them had been closeted together for a couple of hours now. Every time Nicole had ventured out from her office, she'd sent a baleful glare toward her father's closed door and the atmosphere had become so tense it was almost palpable.

The arrival of the junior receptionist from downstairs, bearing the morning's mail and courier deliveries, was a welcome distraction. Anna swiftly sorted the mail and then turned to the courier packages. One in particular, slimmer than the rest, stood out. She lifted it and checked the return address. Her stomach instantly knotted. Marked Private and Confidential and addressed to Charles, it had come from the lab he'd engaged to conduct the DNA testing.

She dropped it on the stack of mail she'd already opened for him, as if it burned her fingers. While he'd authorized her, long ago, to attend to all his correspondence, both personal and relating to the business, she had no doubt he'd want to open this particular item himself.

The door to Charles's office opened and she jumped, feeling as if she'd been caught doing something wrong. Judd's ever-intense gaze swept her body and, obviously noticing her reaction, one dark brow lifted slightly in query. She ignored him, something that she'd wished she'd become more capable of in the past few days. Back in Australia, she'd tried to resist her attraction to him because she'd worried about the backlash when he learned the truth. She'd never realized that there was part of the story that even *she* didn't know—that Charles intended for Judd to take over the company. Once the DNA test results verified what they all already knew, Judd would become her boss.

That *should* make him absolutely off-limits. Her brain was sure of it. Her body, though, was much harder to convince.

Just thinking about him was enough to make her body heat with arousal. Being in the same room as him, even under the same roof, was absolute torture. For the past week, work had been her refuge away from him, but it looked like that wouldn't be the case any longer.

"Anna, I want you to take Judd on a tour of our biggest Auckland stockists, introduce him to the store and chain managers. No need for appointments, hmm? Let's catch them on the hop and see how we're faring against the competition."

"Wouldn't you rather do that yourself?"

Anna couldn't think of anything worse than having to spend the balance of the day solely in Judd's company. While she hadn't been able to fault his behavior toward her since their return to New Zealand, there was an undercurrent that remained ever present between them. An undercurrent that kept her nerves wound so tight she was beginning to wonder if she shouldn't request a leave of absence and head away for a couple of weeks, just to be able to breathe again without constantly thinking of Judd Wilson.

"You know I can't drive myself and we can hardly expect Judd to find his way around on his own just yet."

"It's okay," Judd interceded smoothly. "I'm sure that with a GPS I'll be fine."

"No," Charles insisted, his color rising slightly. "I've asked Anna to take you and she will. Everyone knows her already and it will make the introductions much smoother. Isn't that right, Anna?"

Anna pushed her chair away from her desk and stood,

gathering her handbag from the locked drawer at the bottom of her desk as she did so.

"Sure, Charles. Whatever you want."

"Right, then, that's settled." Charles looked at the pile of newly opened mail on her desk. "Is that lot for me?"

"Yes, I was about to bring it through to you."

She saw his eyes light on the courier package and the ruddy color that had begun to suffuse his cheeks faded rapidly.

"Charles? Are you okay?"

"Stop fussing, woman," he blustered. "Of course I'm fine. You two had better get going. And take Judd somewhere nice for lunch, too. I don't expect to see the two of you back here this afternoon. You have a lot of ground to cover."

Resigning herself to Judd's company for the rest of the day, she passed the mail to Charles and took her car keys from her handbag. She watched Charles head back into his office and slam the door closed behind him. So, they weren't to discover the contents of the courier pack until he was ready to share it with them.

"You really don't have to take me around today if you don't want to," Judd said from close by.

"No, it's okay. Charles wants you to have personal introductions, I understand that." *I may not like it, but I do understand it,* she amended silently.

"Do you always do exactly as he says?"

"Why wouldn't I?" she answered, wondering where Judd was leading with his question.

"No reason, I just thought you might stand up to him a bit more."

"He'd never ask me to do something I truly objected to, if that's what you're aiming at," Anna said defensively.

"That's good, then. You don't object to being with me today. Shall we go?"

He smoothly reached out and placed a hand at the small

of her back, guiding her toward the door. She felt its imprint as if she was naked and hastened to create some distance between them. As his hand fell away, her body instantly mourned his touch and she castigated herself soundly for her ridiculous reaction.

Judd didn't speak again until they drove out from the underground staff car park in her shiny dark red Lexus IS 250 F-Sport.

"Nice car," he commented.

"It's a company car, it has four wheels and gets me where I need to go."

"Kind of pricey for a company car for a P.A. You must be *very* good at your job."

There was an insinuation that hung in the air between them that she really didn't like. But she wouldn't give him the satisfaction of biting back.

"Charles likes to show his appreciation to all his valued staff," she replied, choosing her words carefully.

"Some more than others, I imagine."

Again that prick at her relationship with Charles. She knew many people didn't understand it and she'd learned to shield herself from speculation and unkind comments. It was a skill she'd had to develop early when the children at the private school Charles had paid for had discovered she was his housekeeper/companion's daughter.

Growing up with the stigma of her mother's relationship with Charles hanging over her, and the sly innuendo that had accompanied it, had made her a great deal tougher than she looked. It didn't mean that such comments didn't hurt, not at all, but there was no way she would give the person inflicting it any satisfaction at all, nor would she divulge more information than she absolutely needed to. And never, ever would she let herself be a woman who got physically involved with her boss.

She started giving Judd a rundown on the major chains

that Wilson Wines supplied with imported wines as she drove toward their head office. But he interrupted her almost immediately.

"Who is Wilson Wines' greatest competition?"

"Jackson Importers. Why do you ask?"

"In any venture, it always pays to know who you're up against. Tell me about them."

"They were set up just over twenty-five years ago by Thomas Jackson. He died about a year ago and the company is now headed by Nate Hunter. He's about your age and he's been with Jackson since graduating with a business degree from Auckland Uni. That's pretty much all we know about him. He's been working out of one of their overseas offices for most of his career and has only recently come to New Zealand to take the reins from the interim CEO. No one's really too sure what he's like personally. What we do know is that he has a very competitive business head on his shoulders and he works hard to give us fierce competition. He's run their European operations superbly for the past few years."

"Thomas Jackson...I think I remember someone with that name from when I was a kid."

"That would probably be right," Anna commented. "Thomas Jackson and your father were business partners and best friends. They had a disagreement and Charles bought him out."

"Must have been a helluva disagreement."

"I wouldn't know." Anna shrugged, trying to keep her face expressionless. "It was before my time and my mother never spoke about it." True, her mother hadn't spoken about it, and neither had Charles—but Anna had drawn her own conclusions from the rumors that still persisted even years later, and it wasn't difficult to do the math. Charles's divorce from Cynthia and his falling-out with Thomas Jackson had happened at exactly the same time. Those incidents coupled with Charles's insistence on Judd being DNA tested—well, the writing was very clearly on the wall.

Judd sat in his seat, a contemplative expression on his face. Anna wondered what on earth was going through his mind.

"Charles has never said anything to you about it?" he eventually said.

"Not a word, and it's not really something I'd raise with him, anyway. If you want to know more, you'll have to speak to him yourself," she said a little sharply.

Judd chuckled. "And so I'm duly put firmly in my place."

"I didn't mean—"

"Don't worry, Anna. You're right. I should do my own background checks if I want to know things. And I will."

His words made her nervous. Why was it so important for him to dig into the past? Surely it was enough that his father wanted to mend the broken bridges between them. She knew that the death of Thomas Jackson had hit Charles hard. She'd always thought Charles had thrived on the challenge and competition his past colleague presented to him on a regular basis, but now she wondered whether, once the heat and anger had died down, Charles hadn't been suffering regret for the way their friendship had ended.

Either way, the topic wasn't open for discussion as far as she was concerned. She swung her car into a space in the car park at the premises of Wilson Wines' largest customer, grateful for the opportunity to put some space between them. Knowing his opinion of her had done nothing to calm her ever-present awareness of him—of the way her body warmed every time he was in the vicinity, of her hyperawareness of his alluring cologne as it wreathed her senses in forbidden enticement. She resolutely cleared her mind of anything else but what Charles had asked her to do today. She'd get through this, even if it was the last thing she wanted to do.

Six

The minute they set foot back in the house Anna could sense something in the air. There was an energy thrumming through the place that hadn't been there this morning and when she went through to the kitchen for a chilled glass of water, the cook and housekeeper were working flat out on what looked to be very elaborate meal preparations.

"Did I miss something?" she asked the cook, who was busily checking pots on the commercial-size stove top.

"No, dear. Just himself making requests for something very special for dinner tonight—says he has an important announcement to make, and he wants you all to dress up, too. Can you let Miss Nicole know when she gets in?"

Clearly the courier pack he'd received this morning had borne the news Charles had wanted so very much. A vague numbness permeated Anna's body, leaving her confused about how she felt about the news. It was what Charles had wanted, there was no doubt about that. But she knew he hadn't said a word yet to Nicole about his plans. If he had, she knew Nicole would have discussed it with her. Still, Nicole had been avoiding her lately, still stung, Anna was sure, over her not disclosing the reason for her trip to Adelaide. Worried she might miss Nicole, she sent her a text message.

Don't be late tonight. Your dad wants us all dressed up for dinner. He has an announcement to make. —A.

Nicole was quick to reply; a series of question marks flashed across Anna's screen. She swallowed against the knot of disloyalty that tightened in her throat as she texted back.

No idea what it's about, sorry.

On the way to her room she passed by Charles's suite, knocking softly on the door before letting herself in. He wasn't in his private sitting room, so she figured he must be resting. It had become a regular habit of his after a half day at the office—late starts, early finishes and plenty of rest in between. She was reluctant to disturb his nap, but she needed to talk to him about Nicole. Deciding to wait until she heard him up and about in the bedroom, she settled on one of the comfortable sofas he had in the sitting room and popped her feet up beside her.

Some time later Anna stirred at the sound of running water coming from the other room. She blinked to clear her eyes, realizing it had grown full dark outside. She dragged a hand through her hair. It was sticking every which way. Darn, she knew she should have tied it up today. A quick glance at her watch revealed how close it was to the dinner hour. There was no way she'd be able to be ready and talk to Charles this side of dinner. As it was, she'd be pushing it to get ready on time.

She shrugged out of her jacket, tucking it under one arm, and untucked then started to unbutton her blouse as she headed for the door. She opened it and slipped outside into the hallway, only to come face-to-face with Judd. Her nostrils flared, taking in the freshly showered scent of him.

"If you'll excuse me," she said, trying to sidestep past him and get to her room, "I'm running late."

Judd's expression, usually distinctly unreadable, reflected a look of surprise, before a cold, calculating look appeared in his eyes.

"So I see," he said, stepping to one side to let her by.

Understanding dawned with the drenching effect of sub-Antarctic waters. "It's not—"

"Didn't you say you were running late?" he reminded her with that arch to his brow that he used with such great effect.

Without another word she stalked past him to her room a little farther down the hall. She closed the door behind her and leaned against the solid wooden surface, realizing that she was shaking. There was no question that Judd thought he'd caught her *in flagrante delicto*. Anna pushed herself away from the door and forced herself to walk through to her en suite bathroom, peeling the rest of her clothes off on the way. What should it matter what Judd Wilson thought? It wasn't the truth, so as far as she was concerned it shouldn't matter one iota. Even so, as she stepped beneath the spray of her shower, she couldn't help wishing she hadn't put that look of disapproval on his face.

By the time she'd dressed, reapplied her makeup and swept her hair up into an elegant chignon, she'd missed predinner drinks. She joined Charles, Judd and Nicole as they walked through to the dining room. Despite her text to Nicole, her friend obviously hadn't had time to change out of her work clothes—or perhaps had chosen not to, knowing it would rile her father.

"Sorry I'm late," Anna said breathlessly as she entered the dining room.

"You're here in time for the important news," Charles said with a thread of emotion in his voice that put Anna's nerves on edge.

She took her seat, opposite Judd, feeling the blue fire of his gaze upon her as she did so.

"What important news?" Nicole asked.

Anna felt her throat close and her chest tighten. This wasn't going to be pretty. As dependable as Nicole was in a business setting, she wasn't known for deliberation or contemplation when it came to her private affairs. Impulsiveness and impetuosity were more her mark in trade. She wasn't going to take the news of her father's plans happily. Especially not when she'd worked so hard at his side all these years, striving constantly to be everything he needed in business and in family.

Charles seemed oblivious to Anna's distress and to the storm that was brewing. He was puffed up with pride. Anna hadn't seen him this animated in some time. He picked up his glass and gestured in Judd's direction.

"I'd like to propose a toast. To my son, Judd. Welcome home, where you truly belong."

Anna hazarded a look at Judd, watching to see if this open declaration that he was definitely Charles's son would have an effect on him at all. She was disappointed. He merely nodded toward his father and raised his own glass in response.

"Aren't you repeating yourself, Dad?" Nicole asked. "Didn't we already go through this last Friday when Judd arrived?"

"No, I'm not repeating things at all. It is a relief to an old man to be able to acknowledge his family, *all* his family, now that the results have come in. And to that end I have a small presentation to make."

Charles patted a long, narrow envelope that sat on the tablecloth next to his place setting. He picked it up and handed it to Judd.

"You'll find it all in there, son. Exactly as I promised."

Even though he knew there had never been any doubt about his paternity, Judd felt a thrill of exhilaration surge through him. Here it was, the moment he'd been waiting for,

for most of his adult life. His father handing him the tools with which to pay him back for what he'd done to Judd and his mother all those years ago. Tomorrow he would have a solicitor draw up the share-transfer papers in order for him to present Nate Hunter with an offer that the man could not refuse. The controlling interest in Wilson Wines for the princely sum of one dollar. Judd took the proffered envelope.

"Thank you, sir."

"Oh, surely you don't have to call me 'sir,'" Charles blustered. "If you can't call me Dad, then at least call me Charles."

"Thank you, Charles."

He saw the hope in his father's eyes dim a little. There was no way he could call this man "Dad," not after all these years. He scanned the two women at the table. Anna sat there, frozen, as if she was expecting something terrible to happen and she was totally helpless to prevent it. He began to get some understanding of the reason why when he saw his sister's face.

Confusion battled with irritation across her features and it didn't take long before she was demanding some clarity about what had just been passed over to him.

"What did you promise, Dad?" she asked, a fine tremor in her voice betraying her heightened nerves.

"Only what Judd has always been due, Nicole."

She flung a dark-eyed glare at Judd. "And that would be?"

"The deed to the house and a controlling interest in Wilson Wines. The rest will go to you on my death, as you well know," Charles interjected. "Now, shall we have another toast and get down to the business of enjoying the wonderful meal I know Mrs. Evans has prepared?"

"A controlling interest in Wilson Wines?" Nicole's voice rose on a note of incredulity. "Dad, what are you doing? He doesn't know the first thing about the business."

"He has experience with the wine industry in Australia.

And now that he's home, he has time to learn how we do things here," Charles said, as if that was the end of the matter.

"That's not fair. I've given everything to Wilson Wines, to *you*. And you just go and give it all away, just like that. To a stranger?"

"He's your brother, he's not a stranger," Charles snapped back, the color in his cheeks an unhealthy ruddy red.

"He may as well be."

Judd felt he should say something, but he held back. When he followed through on his plans for Wilson Wines, his sister would be glad she didn't know him better and would probably never even want to see him again, anyway. The knowledge gave him a sharp pang of regret. They'd both been cheated of so much by their father's dictatorial decisions. Maybe he'd be able to find her something to do within The Masters'.

Across the table, Nicole laughed, but the sound held no humor in it. Anna reached out and took Nicole's hand in hers, squeezing it tight, but Nicole shook her off, turning on her instead.

"You're just as bad. I suppose you knew about this?"

Anna's expression told his sister all she needed to know.

"I can't believe it. Betrayed by the only two people in the entire world that I love." She pushed her chair back from the table and rose. "I can't stay here and listen to any more of this. It's just wrong."

"Nicole, calm yourself and sit down," Charles interjected. "This is how things should have been all along. You know it as well as I do. I never made you any promises about Wilson Wines. Just you wait, you'll find some young man who'll sweep you off your feet and before I know it you will be married and raising a family. Wilson Wines will just be a hobby for you."

Judd might not know his sister well, but even he could tell that that had been the dead-wrong thing to say. "A hobby?" Nicole's voice rose steadily. "I can't believe this. You can't be

serious. Wilson Wines is everything to me. I love the business, love the industry—everything I learned was so I could
run the company one day. I've lived under the same roof as
you all my life, worked beside you every day I possibly could
to try and earn your respect, and yet you don't know me at
all."

She made for the door. Anna rose and went after her.

"No, let me go!" Nicole said, tears tracking down her
cheeks as she held up her hands as if to ward Anna off.

Judd could see the hurt in Anna's eyes, the guilt she clearly
felt for not having given Nicole any warning of what her
father had been about to do. Even he felt sick to his stomach
that his father could so cavalierly shrug off Nicole's contri-
bution to Wilson Wines in the past few years and denigrate
it as a hobby. Another black mark in the increasing collec-
tion against Charles Wilson.

"She always was a little high-strung," Charles commented
as Nicole slammed the dining room door behind her. "She'll
come around, you'll see. She doesn't have it in her to stay
angry for long."

"Charles," Anna said, "this is more than a tantrum. Can't
you see? You've hurt her deeply."

"Do you think so?" Charles cast her a look of genuine surprise. "No, she's just being overemotional, that's all. She'll
calm down soon and see this is all for the best. I've always
had her best interests at heart, you know that."

"Do I?" Anna pressed. "Don't you think she sees it as her
position within Wilson Wines being undermined, let alone
her position here in her home?"

Judd had to admire the way she stuck up for his sister.

"Don't be ridiculous. She'll always be my daughter. In
fact, I've probably spoiled her over the years. She'll just have
to get used to the idea of sharing with Judd now, is all. Now,
come and settle back down. Mrs. Evans is waiting to serve."

"I need to make a call—to make sure she's okay," Anna insisted.

Charles waved a hand. "Fine, then, go ahead. Do what you must."

When Anna returned, Charles rang the small crystal-and-silver bell that stood beside his water glass. Judd watched as Anna resumed her seat, her body vibrating with tension and her distress clear on her features. The call to his sister can't have gone well.

Anna excused herself from the table immediately after dessert, leaving Charles and Judd to talk, but it wasn't long before Charles showed signs of weariness and also left to go upstairs to bed.

Alone? Judd wondered, his mind uncomfortably casting back to when he'd surprised Anna coming from the older man's suite of rooms. She'd clearly been in the process of putting her clothes back on in case someone saw her in the hallway. And someone had. Judd's hand tightened on the stem of the Waterford crystal goblet in his hand, the glowing red wine within it barely touched.

Well, he could certainly find out if she had gone ahead to warm his father's sheets. All it would take would be an inquiry at her door.

Judd barely realized he'd made the decision to check on Anna until he found himself outside of her bedroom. He raised his hand and rapped softly on the door, leaning one shoulder against the jamb as he waited for it to open. To his surprise, it did.

"What do you want? To gloat?" Anna asked him.

For a moment, he was taken aback but he soon recovered his usual equilibrium and took a moment to savor the scrubbed freshness of her face and her hair loose in a well-brushed tumble across satin-covered shoulders. The shadows cast by the soft lighting in her room showed she wore very little beneath her robe. If anything. Instantly he was rock hard, his body clamoring with an urgent need to possess her. He stamped down on the sensation. So she wasn't with Charles now, but she had been earlier this evening. The image of her, fresh from his father's room, still burned in his memory, and he fought the urge to create a new memory—one of his making.

He gathered his thoughts together and expelled a harsh breath before speaking. "Not at all. It should have been handled differently."

She made a sound, a cross between derision and a cynical laugh. "You think? You know you could have asked him to consider Nicole's feelings before making that stupid announcement."

"Mea culpa," he said, straightening from the door frame and holding his hands wide. "It didn't occur to me that he wouldn't have told her privately."

"Well, it's too late now. Hopefully we can sort things out at the office tomorrow, if she's talking to me again by then. What did you come to see me for, anyway?"

"I wanted to make sure that you were okay. You looked upset at dinner."

She looked at him in surprise. "Upset? In being loyal to Charles I betrayed my best friend since I was five years old. Of course I'm upset."

"Why did you do it? Why does he have such an influence over you?" Judd persisted.

"You would never understand," Anna said and started to close the door.

Judd put out a hand to halt its traverse across the plush carpet.

"Try me."

"Look, it's late. I don't want to talk about this now. What's done is done." She stared pointedly at his hand and then back at his face. "Good night, Judd."

He took the hint and removed his hand from the door.

"Sweet dreams, Anna."

But he was talking to a plank of painted wood. So, he thought as he walked back to his room, she didn't want to discuss her relationship with his father. How surprising, not. He was prepared to leave it—for now—but eventually he'd get the truth from her. In the meantime, he'd do his best to imprint his own influence. Whatever her feelings for Charles, the attraction between Anna and himself was mutual—her capitulation would be a sweet success.

The next morning, Anna waited patiently for Nicole to come into the office, but she didn't show. Repeated calls to her cell phone resulted in no response. Charles hadn't come into the office today, either, and according to the household staff, Judd had remained closeted with him back at the house. Anna didn't like the way this was panning out.

She stifled a yawn and decided to take her morning break a little earlier than usual. Maybe a shot of caffeine would help her get through to lunchtime. In the staff lunch room she grabbed her favorite cup from the shelf and headed for the coffee machine. One of the office staff sat at the table, nursing her own cup of coffee and scanning her laptop screen. As Anna passed by she caught a glimpse of the page the girl was on and smiled. The anonymous celebrity-gossip column in the print and online newspaper usually made for a humorous read.

"Anything good in there today?" she asked, sitting down at the table with the other girl.

"The usual, mostly. Oh, wait. Look at this!"

She swiveled the computer around so they could both view the screen. Anna scanned the text, when her eyes were suddenly arrested by a name—Nicole Wilson. The comments about Nicole focused mostly on her being seen letting her hair down in one of the city's bright spots the night before and, in particular, with a certain extremely eligible and wealthy

Auckland businessman who was newly returned to town to take over control of a major company. While his name wasn't mentioned, there was only one person that Anna knew fitted the carefully worded description. Nate Hunter. A photo accompanied the article. While her partner's back was to the camera, there was no mistaking Nicole in fine form on the dance floor.

Somehow Anna managed to say the right things to the other girl and made her way back to her office, her rapidly cooling coffee clutched in her hand.

What on earth should she do? she wondered. She had to get a hold of Nicole and find out what she was up to—but how? She did a quick search online, and found the number for Jackson Importers. Maybe Nate Hunter might be able to shed some light on where Nicole was.

Five frustrating minutes of being stonewalled later, Anna replaced the receiver on her phone. Mr. Hunter was unavailable until further notice. What that meant, exactly, Anna had no idea, but she had the sinking feeling that wherever Nicole was, it was very possibly with him. And given her mood last night and her tendency to be outrageously impulsive, it didn't augur well.

Darn Judd Wilson, she thought, and darn Charles, too. This was all their fault. Anna clenched her hands into fists and fought back the urge to scream. One by one she uncurled her fingers and released her fury on a pent-up breath, then reached for her phone and dialed Judd's number. They needed to swing into damage control before all this blew up in their faces. He'd know what to do.

Seven

"It's preposterous. What on earth is she thinking?"

Anna winced as Charles raged through the office on Monday afternoon after what had been an exceptionally stressful and long weekend waiting for his prodigal daughter to return home. She knew all the anger and tension couldn't be good for him, but there was nothing she could do to calm him down when the bad news about Nicole kept pouring in. The latest update—that she'd turned up for work at the offices of Jackson Importers late that morning—had gone down like a lead balloon.

He continued his rant. "She isn't thinking, that's what. And she wonders why I gave the controlling interest in Wilson Wines to Judd."

"She's hurting, Charles. Give her time, she'll come back." Anna tried to soothe his anger but it was useless.

"Come back? I wouldn't have her back. Not now that she's working for that insufferable miscreant! I've a good mind to cut her out of my will completely after this." Anna wanted to believe he was just blowing off steam, but she had a sinking feeling that he meant every word. Nothing made Charles angrier than what he perceived as disloyalty. No matter what excuse she offered, Anna was pretty sure that Charles wouldn't be forgiving Nicole in a hurry.

"And what are we supposed to do in the meantime, hmm?" Charles continued. "We needed her here to help transition Judd into his duties. Now he's dropped in at the deep end."

"I'm sure I'll cope." Judd interrupted his father's tirade. "I'm not completely unaware of how a business should be run nor am I unfamiliar with the wine industry."

Anna looked at him and felt that familiar tug of attraction she'd fought all weekend to ignore. It was hard enough to resist him under normal circumstances, but over the past weekend, when Anna had felt that her whole world was collapsing around her, Judd had been a rock—stepping right in to make sure everything was taken care of. While Anna had been busy keeping Charles reined in and ensuring that his riled temper didn't prevent him from keeping up with his medical treatments, Judd was the one who'd handled the reporters' phone calls, coordinated with the company's PR team and ensured that all Wilson Wines employees, particularly those who reported directly to Nicole, were reminded of the nondisclosure agreements they had signed.

He'd single-handedly kept the disaster from spiraling out of control. While Anna couldn't help but be grateful to him, she was forced to admit to herself that it was entirely unfair how attractive he was when he was coolly, competently in charge.

Today he looked every inch the high-powered executive, wearing a navy suit and crisp white shirt with a patterned tie. He could have stepped off the pages of a men's fashion magazine, and yet despite the polish, there was still that edge of visceral male that hovered about him.

"Anna?" Charles's voice. "Are you paying attention?"

"S-sorry," she stuttered. "I was woolgathering."

Charles sighed heavily. "I need you to be on your game, young lady. Without Nicole here, I'm appointing you as Judd's P.A. He's going to need the support of someone who knows Wilson Wines from the ground up. You're the only one I trust for that role."

"His P.A.?" Her heart gave an uncomfortable lurch. "But what about you?"

"I'm sure you can draw on one of the girls from marketing to help me when I need it. That redhead who covers for you when you're on holiday, she'll do. It's not as if I'm in here for full days, anyway…although I suppose that will have to change now Nicole's gone."

He suddenly slumped in his chair, his face gray. Anna rushed to his side.

"Are you all right? Do you need the doctor?"

Charles shook his head. "No, don't fuss, Anna. I'm not sick. Not physically, anyway. It just isn't right. I finally get Judd back and I lose Nicole."

Anna fought the urge to tell him she'd tried to warn him that what he was doing would drive a wedge between himself and his daughter. She found consoling words instead to replace the ones that hung bitterly on the tip of her tongue.

"You haven't lost her, she'll be back before we know it, I'm sure."

"In the meantime, you have us," Judd commented. "And speaking of which, I think you should head home and rest and leave the running of the office to Anna and me. We can call you if anything arises that we can't manage."

Anna felt a burst of cold panic at the thought of her and Judd alone together in the office, but still, she found herself agreeing with him. Anything to see to Charles's comfort. After the older man had been driven home by his new temporary P.A., Anna showed Judd into Nicole's office. Charles had stipulated that he should work from there, and while a little voice inside of her had objected vociferously, she accepted the practicality of it. If Judd was to assume Nicole's duties quickly, he needed information to be at his fingertips. Where better than in Nicole's office?

It was lunchtime when he came out and over to Anna's desk.

"I see Nicole had a trip planned to Nelson, leaving on Thursday. I thought Wilson Wines primarily imported from overseas markets."

"We do, but Nicole campaigned to introduce several wines from New Zealand to our catalogue as well, with a view to distributing only to select wine sellers and collectors. She felt it was a strong counter to Jackson Importers' ability to cut prices by dealing through the internet. This way we'd have top-quality wines but without the additional costs involved with importation."

Judd nodded. "Makes good sense. So this project is still in its infancy?"

"Yes, she's already visited a few North Island wineries. This week was to source specific wines from the top of the South Island."

"You'll need to change her tickets to my name and book a set for yourself, as well."

"Me?"

A small frown creased between his eyebrows. "Why not?"

"I don't usually do these trips. My role is more one of support here, at home."

"I need you with me."

"Surely you can—"

"Anna, you're coming with me. We're not departing until early evening on Thursday and will be returning to Auckland on Tuesday morning. The office can survive a few days without you."

"But Charles—"

"Has a new P.A. now. Or had you forgotten that?"

* * *

Judd eyed Anna carefully. He hadn't expected an opportunity to get her alone and to himself quite so quickly but he certainly wasn't going to waste it. Getting her out from under his father's roof and into his own bed had become a task he'd begun to relish. His sister's display of pique had fallen right into his hands. He'd thank her for it one of these days. Probably right about the time he offered his controlling interest in Wilson Wines over to Nate Hunter.

After the weekend's development, he'd shelved his original plans to hand over the company right away. Oh, he still intended to take Wilson Wines apart...but not quite yet. Charles was still reeling from Nicole's actions, and Judd wanted him feeling secure and invulnerable again when Judd struck. Besides, seducing Charles's mistress away from him would be a lot easier when she was forced to work right at his side.

For now, business was the least of his concerns. His sights were very firmly set on the woman in front of him. The woman whose scent, even now, tantalized him. Living under the same roof and not touching her—imagining her with his father—had been torture these past few days. He hadn't seen any overt displays of affection between them, but she'd certainly been hovering over Charles nonstop. Judd also hadn't forgotten her state of dishabille last Thursday evening when he'd caught her coming from the old man's rooms.

Each time he'd had an opportunity, he'd cut her from Charles's attention over the weekend, even going so far as to brush against her from time to time. He knew his touch unsettled her—the faint flush of color on her cheeks had been a dead giveaway—but she'd managed to gracefully extricate herself from each situation and create a distance between them that had left him frustrated both physically and mentally.

This trip to the South Island was a godsend. She would be

his willing lover before they returned, and stage one of his decimation of the things his father loved would have begun.

By the time Thursday morning rolled around Judd felt as if every cell in his body was taut with anticipation over what this trip would bring. He'd done some more research and had personally contacted each of the wineries they were to visit to explain that he was coming in his sister's stead. So far the reception had been promising, as had been the sample wines that Nicole had in her office that she'd received in advance of the trip. He could see why she'd chosen them. They had distinct appeal on many levels. His sister definitely had a strong talent for innovation and combined it with exemplary taste.

The business side of the trip aside, he was looking forward to the concentrated time alone with Anna Garrick. That she very clearly wasn't only made the prospect more appealing and the challenge even more enticing. He still well remembered her response to his kiss that first night at The Masters'. Remembered the feel of her body, her full breasts, the soft curves of her body against his, the taste of her. Damn if he wasn't getting hard just thinking about it.

He walked into the dining room at the house that already felt like home and saw Anna at the sideboard helping herself to cereal and milk.

"Good morning, all ready for the trip?" he asked.

She took her bowl over to the table and sat down before acknowledging his presence.

"Good morning," she said, her voice a little husky as if she'd not long been awake.

The fresh scent of her and her immaculately applied makeup gave lie to the thought that she'd tumbled straight from bed. Add to that the fact that she was dressed smartly in a cream blouse neatly tucked into a pair of taupe-colored trousers that she'd cinched at the waist with a wide black belt, suggested she'd been up for some time. The blouse was made of some sheer floaty fabric that clung to her in all the right places. Beneath it he caught a hint of a lacy camisole. He was going to have to exhibit some control, he decided, if he wasn't to walk around all morning in a state of constant arousal. But there was something so carnally alluring about her, he knew it would be easier said than done.

Anna pushed her cereal around in her bowl, clearly not finding the prospect of breakfast at all tempting. In the meantime, Judd helped himself to some fluffy scrambled eggs and a couple of strips of grilled bacon.

"Are you sure you really need me to come with you on this trip?" she blurted as he sat down and reached for the coffeepot on the table.

"I wouldn't have said so if it wasn't necessary."

She sighed, the action making her breasts rise and fall beneath the gossamer-fine fabric and making his fingers itch to touch it and what lay beneath.

"I really don't think I should be leaving Charles, what with Nicole gone, as well."

Judd felt his resolve harden. "He's an adult and quite capable of taking care of himself."

"But he'll be alone."

"In a house filled with staff? I don't think so. I've spoken with Mrs. Evans already. She'll keep a close eye on him."

"It won't be the same," Anna replied, a mutinous set to her mouth.

He'd just bet it wouldn't be the same. And if he had anything to do with it, it wouldn't be the same ever again. If Anna was going to pay a furtive visit to anyone's room, it would be to his from here on in.

"He'll cope. Mrs. Evans will be staying in and has all the necessary numbers if she needs assistance." He looked at her swirling her spoon in her now-soggy cereal. "Are you going to eat that?"

She looked down at her bowl, a flash of surprise on her features when she saw the mess in there.

"Um, no. I'm not hungry."

"Are you sure? There's no meal service on the flight."

"I'm aware of that. I'll be fine."

"You don't look fine."

She huffed another sigh. "Look, I don't like small aircraft, that's all. But I'll be okay."

"Fifty passengers isn't such a small aircraft. If you're that worried, I can hold your hand for the entire flight. Rest assured, I'll take good care of you, Anna," he said, giving her a look that intimated a whole lot more than hand-holding.

"I think I'll be able to manage without that. Besides, it's more likely that the prospect of being with you for the next few days is what makes me anxious."

She got up and placed her bowl and spoon on an empty tray at the end of the sideboard. Judd stood and blocked her path as she went to walk past him.

"Now, why would that be, I wonder?" He lifted one finger and traced the edge of her lower lip. "Could it be that you're *anxious* to repeat that kiss we shared in Adelaide?"

"N-no, of course not," she refuted.

"Really?" he said softly. "Do you ever think about it?"

She shook her head and he leaned in a little closer.

"I do." He let his hand drop. "And I look forward to the next time."

"There won't be a next time," she said adamantly, nudging past him and heading for the door.

He watched her leave with a small self-satisfied smile on his face. Oh, yes, these next few days would prove very interesting indeed.

Anna shot up the stairs to her bedroom and closed the door firmly behind her as if another barrier could make a difference to the way Judd Wilson made her feel. She rested a hand on her chest, feeling her rapid heartbeat beneath her palm.

He's just teasing me, she told herself. *Playing games like a cat with a mouse. I certainly don't want a repeat of that kiss.*

Liar! her alter ego whispered in her ear. She shook her head to rid herself of the word echoing in her mind and mentally rechecked her luggage for the trip away. She had everything she needed and then some. All of it nondescript and practical, with not a single low-cut neckline or suggestive hemline amongst it all.

Externally, at least, there'd be nothing about her to tempt Judd Wilson. She hadn't been unaware of his presence these past days. In fact, she could almost say she'd been hyper-aware of him. She'd chosen the blandest combinations of clothing she possibly could every single day, and yet, on several occasions, she'd caught him looking at her as if he'd like to eat her all up.

The visual image of him doing just that forced a moan from her constricted throat. The flat of her hand drifted down to her breast, to where her nipple peaked against the fabric. She couldn't deny it. He had a near uncontrollable effect upon her.

Sex. It was just sex. He was a strong healthy male and he hit all her hot buttons. She really needed to get out more, she decided. Meet new people. Maybe when she got back she'd get a hold of one of the guys at work who was always teasing her about a date. Maybe then she would be able to work this aching tension out of her body and inure herself to Judd Wilson's overwhelming magnetism. She'd get onto it the minute they got back, she promised herself. The very second.

Eight

Anna was shattered by the time they made it back to their riverside hotel in Nelson on Thursday night. They'd arrived at Nelson airport just after two in the afternoon and had hopped into their rental car and driven straight out to the first of two vineyards and wineries that they'd visited today.

The visits, and subsequent talks, had gone well. Nicole's dream was being well and truly brought to reality. Anna fought back the pang that her friend wasn't the one actively seeing her idea come into fruition. Still, it couldn't be helped. She'd made it clear that she'd washed her hands of Wilson Wines, her father and, by association, Anna and Judd, as well. It still hurt that her best friend had severed all ties between them so instantaneously, but she had to respect Nicole's decision.

She rubbed wearily at her eyes, feeling as if she had no more control of her life right now than a leaf did, floating on the river outside. Warm fingers closed over her forearm.

"Are you okay?"

Judd. Always Judd. Always right there, in her face, in her space, in her mind. Somewhere along the course of this week she'd begun to depend on him—on his unwavering sense of command and his capable manner. Even Charles had begun to defer to him—something Anna had never believed she'd see in her lifetime. She had to get a grip on herself—to break the spell Judd was so easily waving about her. She opened her eyes and looked pointedly at where his hand made heated contact with the bare skin of her arm.

"You can let go of me. I'm not about to keel over," she said tartly.

"Of course you're not. Here, this is your room key. We have adjoining rooms. I thought we should eat in tonight and then go over the proposals we discussed with John and Peter today."

"And I suppose we *must* do this tonight?"

"It'll pay to iron out any potential kinks early, don't you agree?"

"Sure," she said, resignation in her voice. "I'd like to freshen up a bit before we eat."

"No problem. I'll order for both of us and have it delivered to my room. Just come through the connecting door when you're ready."

When she was ready. That was rich. *How about never,* she thought defiantly. But she knew she would go through to his room to dine with him. She owed it to Charles if no one else. Already rumors had begun to circulate this week about Jackson Importers approaching at least three of Wilson Wines' major European suppliers. They'd had exclusive contracts with those suppliers but they were all coming up for renewal. A fact that Nicole had known only too well. Was she behind this attempt to undermine her own father?

"Sounds good. Give me half an hour."

"There's no big rush. Take an hour if you need it."

"Thanks, I will." Another hour she didn't have to spend in his company was all good as far as she was concerned.

When she let herself into her room, she cast her eyes around, familiarizing herself with the layout. Basic but comfortable, were the first two things that came to mind, until she stepped into the bathroom and saw the spa bath installed against a white-tiled wall. A sound of anticipation mixed with pure pleasure escaped her and, as she ran the bath, she quickly divested herself of her travel-worn clothes.

She lost track of how long she'd soaked until she heard a muffled knocking from the connecting door. She dragged herself from the water and wrapped herself in a towel. A quick glance at the bedside clock confirmed she'd used up her one hour of grace.

"I'll be right there," she shouted at the closed door, and quickly dried herself off.

She unzipped her case and grabbed fresh underwear, the sheer shell-pink panties clinging a little to her skin as she shimmied into them. She hooked up her bra and then padded on bare feet back to the bathroom to apply some moisturizer and to brush out her hair. She wasn't going to the effort of reapplying her makeup, not when she hoped to be in bed— her own bed, and alone—very soon.

Back in the main room she extracted a lightweight, loose-fitting cotton sweater in taupe and a pair of black Capri pants, before shoving her bare feet into a pair of silver leather slides. A long silver chain with a large silver spinner on the end completed the ensemble. There, that should do it, she decided.

Another knock at the connecting door startled her. She reached out and pulled open the door. Her gaze flicked over him as he filled the frame, making her wish she'd waited a few seconds for him to move away before opening the door. He'd obviously had a shower and changed, too, and her nostrils twitched at the light scent of his cologne. His hair was still wet, making it look blacker than black, and his jaw looked freshly shaven. He'd changed into blue jeans and a black T-shirt that clung to his broad shoulders and chest as if it were made for him. Probably was, she thought cynically. He'd never looked anything less than tailor-made this whole time she'd known him.

"You look worth the wait," Judd said smoothly.

"What's for dinner?" she asked, ducking under his arm and moving into his room.

It was the mirror of hers, with the exception of a California king-size bed instead of the queen she had. She swallowed as she tore her eyes away from the expanse of linen, the bed already enticingly turned down for the night.

"I chose two entrées and a shared main from the menu that I thought would complement a couple of the wines we tried today. We can share the entrées or have just one each. Your choice."

The idea of sharing a dish with him, let alone two dishes, was a bit daunting, but Anna reminded herself she was here to work.

"We can share," she said with as much nonchalance as she could muster.

The autumn evening was still surprisingly warm, and the covered dishes on the trolley near the door to the balcony emitted a mouthwatering aroma. A table for two was set on the balcony overlooking the river, a squat white candle burning in a hurricane lamp providing illumination. Altogether it was a shamefully idyllic and romantic setting. She should have insisted on dining in the main restaurant, she thought, as she took her chair and Judd placed the two entrées in the middle of the table between them.

Anna busied herself filling their water glasses, while Judd poured them each a small measure of the pinot gris they'd brought back with them today.

"So, what shall we start with?" she asked, suddenly very hungry.

"Black Tiger Prawns on a bed of noodles with this wine, I think," Judd suggested, lifting the cover off the first plate.

By the time they'd enjoyed their way through the prawns, followed by a sampling of Green Lipped Mussels and then their shared main course of a trio of meats, Anna felt as if she'd eaten enough to feed an army.

"The new Syrah should be very popular, don't you think?" Judd commented as he leaned back in his chair and took another sip of the wine he'd just mentioned.

"Indeed. It's a variety that seems to be growing in popularity here. To get exclusive distribution on this label is going to be quite a coup. Charles will be pleased."

And there he was again, Judd thought. His father, still intruding.

"Why is his approval so important to you?" he asked.

"He's my boss," she answered simply, turning her face away to look at the lights from the marina sparkling on the now-inky dark water that ran alongside the hotel.

"He's more than that, though. Isn't he?"

She sighed. "Yes, he is. He's always been there for me, and for my mother while she was alive. Without him, I wouldn't be where I am today. I owe him a huge debt of gratitude."

He couldn't quite get a handle on it. It was clear by the tone of her voice, and her actions with his old man, that she loved him. But just where did that love lead?

"He's quite a guy," Judd commented, a little of his frustration creeping into his tone.

"The way you say that…" She shook her head. "You don't know him. Not really."

"And whose fault was that?" he said pointedly. "Look, let's not talk about my father, okay? Let's talk about something else."

She stifled a yawn. "I'm sorry, I think I need to turn in. I haven't been sleeping well lately, and we have an early start for the day tomorrow."

"Sure," he said.

She did look tired, he admitted to himself as he rose from the table and walked with her back to the connecting door. But even with the dark rings under her eyes she was intensely appealing. He'd enjoyed sharing dinner with her—her keen insights into the wines had been valuable, and her company had been surprisingly soothing while they ate. But his enjoyment of her companionship hadn't dampened his desire for the evening to end on a far more sensual note. His body tightened as he considered his plans for this time away together, and as she turned to say good-night, he reached out and caught a few strands of her hair between his fingers, twirling them over and over.

Her mouth parted, as if in protest, but the objection never came. He leaned a little closer.

"Don't you ever wonder?" he asked, pitching his voice low and watching her pupils almost consume the hazel irises of her eyes.

"Wonder what?" she asked, her voice that husky whisper that did crazy things to him and sent a heated jolt of need straight to his groin.

Her eyes had fixed on his lips as he spoke. He moved closer still, until there was no more than a hand width separating their faces.

"What it will be like when we kiss again."

"Who said we'll kiss again?"

"Oh, we will. Don't you want to know if what happened the first time will happen again? Whether we could be *that* good again?"

She blinked and drew in a breath, the word *no* beginning to form on her lips. The sound never made it, as he closed the short distance between them, caressing her lips with his—at first gently and then, when she didn't pull away, with more pressure. His fingers tunneled through her hair to cup the back of her head.

The sensation that shuddered through his body was intense. Even more potent than the last time. He stepped closer, aligning his body with hers and wrapping his free arm around her waist, drawing her against him—feeling the heat of her, the softness, and letting her know in no uncertain terms of the strength of his arousal for her. Slow seduction be damned. The contrast between their bodies incited him to want more, to want it all, to want it now.

His tongue traced the seam of her lips, and as she parted them, he stroked it across the tender inner membrane before tasting her deeper. She met his assault with a parry of her own, her hands now clutched in the fabric of his T-shirt, clinging to him, her hips pressed tight against his own. He flexed his pelvis, gently grinding his hardness against her mound. A moan vibrated from deep in her throat and he captured the sound with his mouth.

Her nipples were hardened points against his chest and he knew without a doubt that one kiss would never be enough. His need to possess her overwhelmed everything else—every need, every thought, other than one. He wanted Anna Garrick like he'd never wanted anything in his life before.

Anna fought to clear the fog of desire that clouded her mind but failed miserably. Hot, hungry need clawed through her as Judd kissed her deeply and she kissed him back just as hard. She knew she should pull back, call a stop to this before they went past the point of no return, but somewhere deep inside she acknowledged that they'd passed that point long ago. What would happen now was inevitable. Nothing—not even the vow she'd made to herself for so many years to never have an intimate relationship with her boss—could stop her from giving in. She wondered whether she would still be able to walk away with some pride, with her heart intact, but her feelings for Judd had crossed some unseen line. Even back in Adelaide, she'd been drawn to him in a way she'd never experienced before. She wanted to take this further—to know him better, to *know* him in every meaning of the word.

There was no reason left that was strong enough to convince her that she shouldn't reach out and take what he was offering. No reason at all. And in return she could give in to him. Anna loosened the fists of her hands and skimmed her palms over his muscled chest and down toward the waistband of his jeans. She yanked the cotton fabric of his shirt loose and shoved her hands underneath, desperate now to feel his skin against hers. But it wasn't enough. His skin burned beneath her touch, igniting her to want even more.

The taut coil of desire deep in her womb tightened even more, and between her thighs she felt herself grow swollen and wet with need. Judd loosened his grip on her, using both hands to push aside her sweater. They broke apart momentarily as he swept the garment up and off her body, exposing her to his gaze. He groaned and bent his head to her neck, nuzzling the tender skin behind her ear and leaving a heated trail of kisses along the way to the hollow of her throat.

One hand cupped her breast, his thumb flicking a distended nipple through the sheer lace of her bra. Her legs threatened to buckle beneath her as his mouth traced a bee-line for the tightly beaded nub. He tugged the edge of her demi-cup bra down, exposing her to his hungry mouth and sending a sizzle of pure fire to her core. She clutched at his waist, anchoring herself to him, and arched her back, easing his access to her as he alternately laved and suckled her.

"You taste so good," he said against her sensitive skin. "But it's not enough."

"Not enough?" She could barely manage to get the words past her lips.

"No, I want to taste all of you."

Judd straightened and gently pulled her hands out from

under his T-shirt before he led her back into his room and to his bed. As she watched in silence, he stripped off his shirt and kicked off his shoes. She reached for him and unbuttoned the top buttons of his fly, her knuckles brushing against the unmistakably swollen ridge of his penis. He grabbed her hands with his.

"That's more than I can handle right now," he groaned, pressing one of her palms against his erection. "Can't you feel what you do to me?"

Words failed her. Her entire body was on fire, liquid molten heat that slowly consumed her inside and out. Judd skimmed his hands up to her shoulders and slid the straps of her bra down before reaching behind her and unsnapping the hooks. The garment fell away from her. He stared at her for so long she began to feel self-conscious, but then he lifted his gaze to hers, his eyes glittering.

"You are so beautiful," he said, reaching out one finger and tracing the pink areola that contracted even tighter under his gentle touch.

He unfastened her pants and pushed them down her legs, the black fabric swiftly followed by her panties. He knelt before her, helping her to step out of the wisp of fabric, then let his fingers glide up her legs, over her trembling thighs and pausing for a second to let his fingers brush the moisture that gathered at their apex.

"You feel so hot, so ready for me," he murmured before pressing his lips where his fingers had been.

His tongue darted against her most sensitive spot, teasing and tasting as if she were some decadent dessert to be slowly savored. Anna clutched his shoulders as he increased the pressure of his tongue, as his lips closed over that sweet bundle of nerve endings, as she was hit with a sudden sharp wave of pleasure that radiated from her core and out to her extremities in a crescendo that tore a cry of satisfaction from deep within her.

She could barely stand another moment. Judd rose swiftly to his feet and guided her back onto the bed. Against her overheated body the sheets were a welcome stretch of coolness, but that coolness was soon swamped by the heat of Judd's body as he rose over her.

He'd said she was beautiful but he was far more so. The symmetry of his body, the strength of his muscles, the golden tan of his skin and the heavy maleness of his arousal—each inch perfection in itself, let alone presented to her as whole.

He'd already grabbed a condom from somewhere and sheathed himself.

"I'm sorry," he grunted as he positioned himself between her thighs. "This is going to be hard and fast, but I promise to take longer next time." He eased his swollen length inside her, his face flushed with concentration. "And the next," he said, his voice strained as he thrust forward, "and the next."

Anna rocked her pelvis to meet his every move, her hands clutching his forearms as they braced at her sides, her legs wrapping around his hips. Her body responded to his fierce possession, a delicious tightening of her inner muscles heralding another orgasm. And then she was there, spasms of pleasure heightening in concentration until she thought she might break apart from the sheer strength of them. Judd lunged within her, his whole body shuddering as he, too, reached his pinnacle of completion.

When he collapsed against her, his breathing was ragged, his body still rocked intermittently by tiny tremors. It was several minutes before he withdrew and rolled to one side. He stroked away several strands of her hair that had settled over her face.

"I'll be right back," he murmured.

Anna nodded, too shattered to speak. A delicious lassitude consumed her body and she lay back on the sheets, barely daring to believe what had just happened between them. Judd came back from the bathroom and slid into the bed beside her then gathered her to him, whereupon he made good on his promise to take longer the next time. And the next.

Dawn was breaking when she awoke. She was sprawled across Judd's chest, her legs tangled in his as if she couldn't get close enough to him. The last time they'd made love she'd been poised above him, and in their aftermath she'd collapsed right where she lay. Their lovemaking had left her nearly incoherent. She'd never felt this close to another human being ever before.

In bed, Judd Wilson was a completely different man. Gone was the underlying tension that always kept Anna on edge in the office, wondering what was really going on in his keenly intelligent mind. No, in bed there had been nothing between them, quite literally. No past, no future—only the present.

Anna carefully loosed her legs from between his and levered herself onto the sheets beside him. Judd barely moved, lost in a sleep so deep his face relaxed into lines that made him look so much more approachable than he did on a day-to-day basis—less driven, less ruthless.

In the gray light filtering through the windows she looked her fill and wondered where they would go to from here. She couldn't be angry with herself for breaking her long-standing rule—clearly Judd was a man who could never be resisted for long. But now that they'd started this affair, she didn't know what came next. She didn't want the kind of relationship her mother had had with Charles, which, while it was a deep and loving friendship, had never given her mother the full security of marriage which Donna Garrick had quietly craved. Her mother's quiet acceptance of everything had made Anna angry with her for just *settling* for a half life.

Charles and Donna had been occasional lovers, a fact that was governed partially by his diabetes-related impotence and by the strictures of Donna being in his employ. There'd always been an imperceptible barrier between them. One that neither of them had fully crossed. Anna had always felt that her mother had compromised her own happiness for the sake of that vague relationship. Perhaps her need to provide a home and a quality education for her daughter had driven her, or perhaps, after her husband's death, she wasn't prepared to risk her heart again for a passionate love.

Anna had been five when her father had died unexpectedly, and her mother had been offered the position as Charles's housekeeper. Anna had grown up under Charles's roof lacking nothing materially. Deep inside, though, she knew that she wanted more—the emotional strength that came with being intrinsically linked with another soul being first and foremost on her list.

Judd was the kind of man she'd always believed she'd fall in love with one day. His looks aside, his intelligence and ability to provide made him an exceptionally attractive mate. But he was more than all that. This past week she'd seen so many of his strengths—his ability to calm Charles in the wake of Nicole's defection being a perfect example.

Could she have all she wanted with Judd? Did he feel the same way about love and marriage and building a life together forever? Did he feel the same way about her? She almost laughed in the early-morning gloom. God, she was pathetic. Here she was after one night of mind-blowing sex and already she was marching him down the aisle. She didn't even know for certain how compatible they were in other aspects of life. All she knew was that the moment she'd set eyes on him she'd reacted to him on an instinctive level she'd never experienced before. Bearing the brunt of his anger when he'd discovered her deception over her reasons for being at The Masters' had been painful to bear. But once they'd gotten to New Zealand, things had changed. She'd seen sides of him she hadn't suspected before. And then last night...well, last night had changed everything. Now she knew for certain that she wanted a future with him. But was that what he wanted, too?

Guilt drove a splinter into her thoughts. And what about his relationship with his sister? What about hers? Nicole already thought she'd gone over to the enemy by having represented Charles in Adelaide. If she knew that Anna was now considering getting seriously involved with Judd, she'd be even more angry—even more hurt. A lifetime of friendship shattered for a man she'd known for only a matter of weeks.

And what about Charles? How would he react to all of this? He'd seemed to encourage the two of them to spend time together, but would he approve of them having a real relationship?

Of course, all of that presupposed that a real relationship was what Judd wanted with her in the first place. Did she dare to even ask? So much was at stake—so much could be ruined if this went badly. Her job, her closeness to the people who meant the most to her, nearly everything she had, including the roof over her head in the house she'd lived in for nearly all her life, could all be lost.

She looked over again at Judd's sleeping form. Even now, the urge to touch him was irresistible. In spite of herself, she curled up closer at his side, feeling a little thrill of pleasure when his arms tightened around her.

For now, he wanted her and she couldn't deny that she wanted him. And away from her friends, from the gossips at the office, from Charles, he was too tempting to resist. Things would change when they got back to Auckland. If nothing else, she certainly wouldn't want to engage in anything inappropriate under Charles's roof. But for now…for now, she'd fall back asleep in Judd's arms. She'd worry about the consequences later.

Nine

Judd felt Anna's withdrawal from him grow incrementally larger as they got closer to home. It started at breakfast on the last morning of their trip, where she'd suggested eating in the restaurant rather than in their room as they had the past few days, and it had continued through their final appointments and for the duration of their plane trip to Auckland. Now, it was dark as Evans drove them up to the house and even though she was sitting right next to him, it felt like she was a million miles away.

After Evans had taken their bags inside the front foyer and gone to put the car back in the multicar garage, Judd turned to Anna.

"Will you stay with me tonight?"

"Judd…" She shook her head, not making eye contact.

"Why not?"

Suspicion roiled inside of him. Was it because they'd be under his father's roof? Or maybe it was because she'd be sleeping in Charles's bed tonight. Anger flared hard on the heels of his suspicions. She'd been his, all his, the past three nights. Those nights hadn't been anywhere near enough to sate the hunger he had for her and he damn sure wasn't sharing her—especially not with his father.

"It just wouldn't be right," she said, picking up her weekend bag and starting up the stairs.

"We could be discreet," he heard himself say. "Although you would have to try harder not to scream when I—"

"Don't. Just, please don't," she said, her voice shaking and warm color spreading across her cheeks.

"I only want to give you pleasure, Anna. Nothing more."

Her hazel eyes locked with his, and for a few seconds he thought he had her, but then she shook her head again and turned away up the staircase.

He watched her retreat from the bottom of the stairs, his whole body humming with frustration. Leaving his bag at the base of the stairs, he turned and went through to the salon, reaching for the brandy decanter and splashing a measure in one of the crystal tumblers he'd swept up off an engraved silver tray on the sideboard. He knocked back a generous mouthful of the spirit and relished the burn as it traversed its way down his throat.

She might have refused him tonight, he decided, but he hoped it would be the last time she did so. Anna Garrick had become an addiction he had no desire to shake. He finished the last of the brandy and headed for his room and his frustratingly empty bed.

The next morning Judd watched Anna under hooded lids as she summarized their trip to the South Island to Charles—leaving out what he felt to be the most important details, of course. For all her poise and aloof elegance, she was neither poised nor aloof in bed. No, in bed she was voracious and generous, two qualities he held in high esteem in a lover. After that first night they hadn't bothered with booking two rooms again, spending their days visiting various wineries and their nights exploring every inch of one another's bodies.

And what a body. Full in just the right places, and firm in others. A man could lose himself in her. And he had, over and over again. It had been difficult to keep his hands off her when they took their business meetings, especially when he'd seen the way other men looked at her—drawn to her beauty, her charm, her sharp mind tempered with such inherent sweetness. She was phenomenal in every respect, and it had been all he could do to keep from crowing that she was his.

Or rather, she *had* been his, until they'd returned to Charles.

Sleep had been a long time coming last night in his large empty bed. She'd well and truly gotten under his skin, he admitted. He wanted her now, even as she showed Charles a swiftly cobbled together PowerPoint presentation showing where they believed the company would make gains on the current market with their new trend of stocking domestically produced wines.

Judd shifted in his chair to ease the sudden tightness in his groin, his movement drawing Anna's attention. Her eyes flew to his face, a question in them—he merely smiled in response and narrowed his eyes just a little. She blushed, a totally delightful quality, and a dead giveaway as to her physical state. He let his eyes drop deliberately to where her nipples left the tiniest peaks through her bra and against the fabric of her blouse. He didn't mistake her sharp intake of breath, nor her very deliberate body language when she turned away from him and wrapped up the presentation.

"So, you see, Charles, all in all, Nicole was on the right track."

"Well, she's not now," he grumbled. "So you're both convinced that this is the right way to go?"

Judd rose from his chair. "New Zealand has long held a

strong position on the world stage for its superior-quality wines. Our clientele deserves to be offered the exclusivity of these labels. We'd be foolish not to. And, I would suspect, if we don't act soon, someone else will."

"Jackson Importers, you mean?" Charles asked sharply. "We can't have them upstage us. How soon before we can get these varieties into distribution?"

As Anna smoothly took over the logistics of the proposal, Judd sat back to watch her in action. Yes, she was the whole package, all right. Intelligent, beautiful and sexy as hell. And she was his; she just needed a little reminding of it.

Later, after Charles had left the office for the day, Judd called her back into his office.

"Close the door behind you," he instructed as she came in.

"Is there a problem?" she asked as she sealed off the outer office, leaving them cocooned together.

"Oh, yeah, there's a problem, all right."

"What is it? Is it an issue with the new wines?"

"No, come over here."

She did as he asked, a worried crease in her brow. The instant she was within reach, he drew her to him, one hand sliding up her back to cradle the back of her head. He lowered his lips to hers and took them in a kiss he'd been waiting for since yesterday. It had been only hours and yet he'd missed this physicality between them with an ache that had plagued him all last night and all day long.

She pulled away from him. "Stop. What if someone comes in?"

"I've already instructed that all our calls be held. No one will interrupt us, but if you're really worried…"

A few steps across the carpeted floor and the door was securely locked. Anna turned, her back to his desk, and faced him.

"What do you think you're doing?"

He smiled in response. "What I've been wanting to do since we got home."

He backed her up to his desk, boosting her up onto its surface, and, hitching her, oh, so sensible office skirt up to the top of her thighs, he stood between her legs.

"If you won't stay with me in my room, we'll just have to make do," he whispered as he bent his head to her neck and lavished the sensitive skin there with alternating nips of his teeth and licks of his tongue.

He felt the quiver of longing that rippled through her.

"But we're in the office, people will know," she protested, but he knew her heart wasn't in it.

Even now her hands were at his waistband, unfastening his belt and sliding his zipper down to gain access to his body. As her hands freed him from his boxer briefs he shuddered in response, relishing the silky softness of her fingers as they closed around his hardness and squeezed with just the right kind of pressure.

"No one will know but us," he groaned into her mouth as he reached between her legs and found her hot and wet already.

His fingers eased behind the fabric of her panties, sliding along her slick crease, back and forth, back and forth. She moaned in response and he kissed her again, flicking his tongue within her, mirroring his actions with his fingers. She rocked against him, trying desperately to force him to make contact with that part of her that he knew would send her flying over the edge, but this time he wanted to extend the torture just a little longer.

Somewhere along the line in the past few days she'd become necessary to him, and sleeping without her last night had been something he wasn't in a hurry to repeat. He wanted her to want him so much, to need him so much, that she wouldn't consider sleeping without him again.

He eased her back down on the desk and took his time

with his free hand flicking open the buttons of her blouse. One by one he worked his way down, his knuckles skimming the soft swells of her breasts as he lingered on those in particular.

"Please, Judd. Let's just do this."

"In good time," he answered, but even as he did so he privately acknowledged that he wouldn't be able to control his desire for her for much longer. Even now he ached to be inside her, his erection at an almost painful level.

She'd given up touching him, so mindless as she was now to his touch. He bent and blew a cool breath across the exposed skin of her breasts, noting with pleasure how the skin raised in tiny goose bumps, how her nipples pressed against the smooth cups of her bra. This one had a front clasp, he realized with a carnal smile, and he wasted no time in squeezing the clasp and letting it ping open. It was like peeling open a luscious, ripe and forbidden fruit.

There she was, on his desk, upon the papers he'd been working on before their meeting with Charles, her hair spread in disarray over his notations, her blouse fallen open together with her bra and her beautiful luminous skin exposed to his hungry gaze. Her nipples, the palest of pinks, were tight nubs of arousal.

He bent down to take one taut peak softly between his teeth, rolling the tip of his tongue against the hard bead of flesh. Beneath him, Anna moaned and squirmed, her pelvis rocking hard against his hand, still striving to make contact with that part of him that now drove him almost to madness. And this was madness. Taking her here, like this, on his desk. It was the ultimate foolishness, and the ultimate fantasy all rolled into one.

It was too much for him. She'd get her wish—he couldn't wait any longer. He reached into his pocket and pulled out a condom then pushed his trousers and briefs down. Sheathing himself took only a moment, but even as he did so she watched him with eyes glazed with such passion he almost lost it right there and then. He eased off her panties and let them drop to the floor and then spread her legs wide. He would never lose this image of her from his mind, he thought as he positioned himself at her slick entrance.

She groaned as he pushed inside her, a guttural sound that made his balls tighten and the head of his penis swell even tighter. He reached for her hands, linking his fingers through hers and bending her arms up so her hands were beside her head. She lifted her legs up to wrap around his hips and he thrust inside her again, watching her eyes cloud with the sensations that spiraled through her. She had caught her lower lip between her teeth and he felt her ripple against him as he increased his pace. Her body began to shake and a soft cry escaped her. He lowered his face to hers, taking her mouth and absorbing the sounds she made as she crested the peak of their passion, the spasms of her body wringing a climax from him that took all his strength not to shout with the sheer power of it.

He collapsed over her, his breathing hard and fast, the slick of perspiration making his business shirt cling to his back. Suddenly the incongruity of their situation struck him, and a chuckle bubbled up from deep inside.

"We must look a sight from the doorway, hmm?" he said, nuzzling her neck before nipping her skin ever so lightly.

"I can't believe we did that," she said, loosing her fingers from his and pushing firmly on his chest. "I won't be able to face anyone in the main office after that."

"You won't need to. Let's go home for the rest of the day."

"We can't, there's too much to do."

Judd allowed her to push him away and stepped away from her, allowing her to slide off the desk and begin to straighten her clothing. She bent to pick up her panties and wriggled back into them, then she grabbed a wad of tissues from the dispenser on his desk and put out her hand.

"Here, let me get rid of that," she said as he removed the condom.

"I wondered why Nicole kept tissues on her desk," he said.

Anna shook her head. "I doubt that's why she had them there."

He smiled in response. "You never know." He adjusted himself and pulled his briefs and trousers back up, tucking in his shirt and straightening his tie. "There, now no one will ever know but us."

"But they may well wonder," Anna said dubiously. "I always swore I'd never…"

"Never what?"

"Never leave myself open to gossip."

He frowned. "What makes you think anyone will gossip about us?"

Was she worried about it getting back to Charles? So let it, if that was the case. He'd even go so far as to start the rumor himself if it meant he had her wholeheartedly.

"Just the nature of people. It was tough at first, starting here while Mum was still alive. Everyone knew she'd worked for Charles before she left to get married and everyone had something to say about us living with him after my dad died."

"How did that come about, exactly?" Judd asked, hitching one hip against the desk they'd just made love upon. God, even the briefest memory of what they'd just done and it was enough to put his blood on a slow burn again.

"A whole string of things, really. Poor financial decisions on my parents' part, a bit of bad luck, as well. Dad was killed on the job. He was driving to a sales call when a tanker blew a tire and hit a bridge abutment. Dad couldn't stop in time and hit the wreckage. They said he died instantly. It was all so sudden. Mum went from being a happy, stay-at-home wife and mother to a single parent with no income, a stack of funeral bills and no prospects of the life-insurance payout until all the paperwork surrounding the accident was taken care of. Charles approached Mum to offer help and when he realized what a terrible position we were left in, he offered her work and a home for both of us. I was only five, and too young, and too sheltered, to remember most of it. All I knew was that I got to live in a big house and that I had a built-in playmate."

Judd began to put two and two together. "So you grew up with Nicole?"

"Pretty much like sisters, really. Charles even sent me to the same school as her. He did far more for my mother and me than was due. I owe him a lot."

"So, he and your mother. Were they...close?"

"Were they lovers do you mean?" she asked bluntly. "Only very occasionally, from what I understand. Once, after a particularly nasty bout of bullying at school, I confronted Mum about their relationship. She tried her hardest to be honest with me and said that theirs was more a relationship based on companionship. Perhaps she was a bit too honest, but she wanted me to understand. Apparently, one of the long-term side effects of Charles's diabetes was a constant struggle with impotence. It had affected him for years, probably since before you and your mother went to Australia. But you know, even despite their closeness, Mum was always still very much an employee. When I was younger I used to hate that she allowed herself to be taken advantage of that way—now I see it was a choice she made to keep us both secure."

"So you and he—"

"Charles and I what?"

"Were never lovers?"

A look of horror passed across Anna's face. "No! Never. How could you even think that? He's always been a father figure to me, nothing more, nothing less."

"So that night I saw you coming from his rooms, half undressed—"

"I'd been waiting to talk to him about Nicole. I fell

asleep—on his sofa, in his sitting room. And then when I woke up and realized how late it was, I was in a hurry to get back to my room and hop in the shower so I could get ready for dinner. I can't believe you'd have thought that of me." She crossed her way to the office door and pointedly unlocked it. "I'm going to the ladies' room to get rid of this, and then for the rest of the afternoon I'll be in my office if you need me."

Judd felt momentarily giddy from the swell of relief that coursed through him. She wasn't Charles's lover. Her devotion to the old man was merely like that of a daughter. Hard on the heels of that thought, he realized just how much he'd hurt her with his assumption, and discovered that he was genuinely sorry to have upset her so deeply. He needed to make amends.

"Anna?"

She hesitated. "Yes?"

"Look, I'm sorry. I jumped to the wrong conclusions. Let me make it up to you. Stay with me tonight and I'll show you just how much."

She shook her head emphatically. "No, whatever you might think of *me*, I won't disrespect Charles that way."

Without saying another word she swung open the door and stalked off. Judd watched her until she was out of his line of sight before crossing around to the other side of his desk and realigning his paperwork. She hadn't exactly embraced his apology, but at least she hadn't closed the door on them both completely, either. It was time to rethink his strategies with respect to his father and to Anna. One thing he remained certain of—he wanted Anna Garrick for himself—no matter the consequences.

Anna spent the rest of the day at work in a state of total turmoil. Was she destined to be her mother's daughter after all? Was this what it had been like for Donna with Charles? That all he had to do, when he wanted to, was beckon his finger and Donna had been his for the taking, just as Anna just had been with Judd? She'd told herself that their interludes during their trip had been a fluke, that once they got back to Auckland, it would be back to business as usual, but when he'd touched her in the office, she hadn't been able to resist.

Her body still thrummed with the aftereffects of her orgasm, making it difficult to concentrate. That, along with the disbelief and shock that she'd allowed herself to be coerced into making love with Judd in his office, and on his desk no less. She'd have a few bruises tomorrow, no doubt. Her own participation in the event had hardly been that of a submissive.

She'd never been incapable of refusing a man before. She'd been selective with her sexual partners—civilized. This thing with Judd was most definitely not civilized. It was earthy sensuality at its most basic level and it had been, oh, so very good. Even now she wanted him again—but at least this time rationality prevailed. Saying no to him had been driven by her respect for Charles. She smiled at herself. Ironic, it was her respect for the very man who'd made her lose a measure of respect for her mother that now governed her choices and decisions. A psychologist could no doubt have a field day with that.

But there it was. It was how she felt. Charles hadn't had to be a mentor for her in her youth, nor had he been obliged to continue to provide a home for her after Donna had died. Yet he'd been a rock for her. Now she owed it to him to be that rock for him, which—for her, at least—meant not sleeping with his son under his own roof.

It stung that Judd could have thought that she and Charles were having an affair. She shuddered. Nothing could have been further from her mind, or Charles's, she had no doubt. But what would have made him think that?

What, or who?

A niggle of doubt emerged from the back of her mind. Something just wasn't right and she couldn't figure out what or why. But there were so many other things on her mind just now that it was easy to dismiss it.

The next few days kept her very busy in the office. Following up with the wineries they'd visited and processing exclusivity contracts with them, making sure every *i* was dotted and every *t* crossed, was the kind of work she welcomed. Right up until four out of the six wineries they'd sent contracts to sent them back with a note saying they'd received another offer of distribution that they had decided to accept.

Four phone calls later and Anna was feeling sick to her stomach. Jackson Importers had apparently aggressively wooed away the business that she and Judd had thought was in the bag. She wasn't looking forward to sharing the news with Judd or Charles.

As expected, Charles was apoplectic.

"How dare she? I can't believe a daughter of mine would stoop so low as to steal business from her father."

"I hate to point this out," Judd said, "but it was her idea all along. By the looks of things, these people's loyalty sat with Nicole rather than with Wilson Wines. It's my fault for not anticipating this might happen."

"Your fault? Rubbish. She's doing this to spite me."

"Maybe," Judd agreed, "but maybe she just followed through with her new boss on an idea she felt had merit. Did you ever give her credit for coming up with this?"

Anna sat back in her chair, stunned into silence. What was this? Judd championing Nicole? Up until now they'd barely discussed Nicole at all. Anna had assumed that Judd felt the same animosity toward her that Charles did, and had been careful not to bring her up. But to hear him supporting her ideas and giving her props for following them through, that was something Anna had never anticipated from him.

"Of course not, it was her job. She did it competently."

"A little more than competently, I would say," Judd observed, a note of censure in his voice that Anna found herself in total agreement with.

Charles had often been strict with his daughter. He had sheltered her, yes—in that respect he'd taken his responsibilities as a father most seriously. But Anna had seen how being the older, single parent of a beautiful, headstrong daughter had left him feeling that he had to be firm, set high expectations and offer limited praise in order to keep her from running wild.

It probably hadn't helped that he had been so busy with business concerns. Anna knew that Nicole had devoted herself so completely to Wilson Wines in the hopes of winning her father's approval, but it had seemed to add even more tension to their relationship. Charles never grew comfortable straddling the line between boss and father, and had been rather too hard on Nicole in his attempts to avoid showing favoritism. Plus, his old-fashioned attitudes about women in the workplace had been a constant source of irritation between them.

The end result was that Charles had stifled Nicole's adventurous spirit to a point where Anna's friend had often complained to her that she felt her opinions meant nothing to him. Charles did love Nicole, but Anna had always felt as if he struggled with how to show it—and frequently made things worse by saying the wrong thing. In fact, as she'd grown older, it had occurred to her that he may even have actively fostered their friendship so that he could use her as something of a go-between with him and Nicole—someone who could understand both of them and carry messages back and forth without causing offense.

"Well, you'll just have to do it better, my boy. I know you can do it. Let's show Jackson Importers that we're made of sterner stuff. Forget about mounting this New Zealand–based initiative."

"And the wineries who have decided to contract with us, what about them?"

"We'll use them as a test on the market. Could be a flash in the pan—who knows. If it's worth developing further, we'll look into it when the figures start coming in. In the meantime, what about expanding our range of Californian wines?"

After their meeting, Anna went back to her office to create a list of potential contacts for Judd to follow up on based on Charles's directives. She was just checking her email when a message came in that she wasn't expecting to see. Nicole. The subject header was blank, giving her no insight into what the other woman wanted. Feeling as if a thousand eyes watched her, Anna opened the message, her eyes scanning the contents quickly. Her friend wanted to see her, was begging her, in fact. She said she'd meet Anna at a waterfront restaurant in Mission Bay at one o'clock. That was in about ten minutes' time. She could make it from their Parnell offices if she left right now.

Anna chewed her lip. She'd missed Nicole terribly, but the choice her friend had made to join Jackson Importers put them on opposite sides, yet how could she refuse her longtime best friend's request?

The accusations Nicole had flung at her before leaving that awful night had hurt—mostly because she knew she'd deserved them. Loyalty to Charles aside, it had always been her and Nicole. She should have found some way to have given her friend prior warning of the bombshell that was about to be dropped on her life. No doubt Charles would be dead set against her seeing Nicole, but bolstered by Judd's clear support of his sister earlier, Anna reached her decision and fired a response back—*I'll be there.*

Ten

Judd sat in his office and realized that the feeling he'd been carrying around with him for the past several days was happiness. Assuming control of Wilson Wines had turned out to be just the kind of challenge he needed. The pressure being put on them by Jackson Importers gave him an appetite to succeed where his father had failed. Strangely, though, handing Wilson Wines to Nate Hunter on a platter didn't hold quite the appeal he had thought it would anymore. He shook his head slightly. Where was that inner fire that had burned deep down inside all these years? Where was the urge to inflict upon his father a measure of the pain the older man had inflicted upon him? He must be going soft.

Of course, there was still the matter of the house. His mother had emailed him, asking when she could visit and put her redecorating schemes into action. He'd put her off for now, but he knew she wouldn't be held back for long. How Charles would handle being under the same roof as his ex-wife was another matter. Judd had noticed his father tiring in the past week. The half days he was spending in the office were taking a toll but, in typical Charles-like manner, the older man had waved aside Judd's concerns and had flat-out laughed at Judd's suggestion that his father cut back to perhaps only three, or maybe four, half days a week until he was feeling stronger. His father was nothing but stubborn— a trait, he acknowledged, he also shared.

He glanced over the report Anna had left on his desk earlier this morning, barely even seeing the words. Stubbornness didn't just run in the Wilson family. Anna Garrick had her fair share of it, as well. While it had given him no small amount of pleasure to know she wasn't his father's mistress, she still refused to sleep with him under his father's roof. She was nothing if not principled, but it was enough to drive a man to rent a hotel room.

Judd flicked back through the report again. Something didn't make sense. Ah, there it was, it was missing a page. It wasn't like Anna to make a mistake like this. Maybe frustration was eating her up inside, too. And maybe he could persuade her that a hotel room at lunchtime was a good idea.

With a smile on his face, he went through to Anna's office. He cursed softly under his breath—it looked like he'd just missed her. Through her office window he caught a glimpse of a flash of red as her car headed out the office car park and down toward The Strand. He'd have to find the page of the report in her computer himself.

He reached for her mouse and brought her flying-asteroid-ridden screen back to life. Uncharacteristically, she'd left her email account open. Judd went to minimize the window but his sister's name caught his eye. What on earth?

He double clicked on the email and read its contents before flicking to the sent-items folder and seeing what Anna had said in return. Without stopping to get the page he needed from the report, he went and grabbed his car keys before heading out the office. They'd suspected Nicole of following up on her earlier contacts in the Nelson wineries debacle, but what if it had been something else entirely? What if it had been Anna who'd fed his sister the information she'd needed to usurp Wilson Wines all along?

A part of him didn't want to believe it could be true. She was doggedly loyal to Charles—but she'd been vociferous in her support of Nicole, too. Wasn't that what she'd been trying to do the night he'd seen her leaving Charles's rooms? Attempting to defend his sister? A sister she was closer to than he probably ever would be, he acknowledged with an unexpected pang of regret. He had to see for himself what they were up to.

The drive to Mission Bay didn't take long and Judd luckily had no trouble finding a parking spot in the first car park area at the city end of the beach. As he strolled toward the old stone building that housed the restaurant mentioned in Nicole's email, he saw Anna's car also parked nearby. He could just wait here in the sunshine, he thought, and ask her when she returned to her car, but a piece of him wanted to watch the two women together.

He stepped inside the restaurant, his eyes taking a moment to adjust to the darker interior from the autumn sunshine outside. He spied Nicole and Anna immediately in the corner near the back of the restaurant and allowed the maître d' to guide him to a table not in their immediate line of sight but from where he could still observe the two women.

"I ordered for us already," Nicole said, as Anna settled in the chair opposite.

"Thank you, I think."

"Oh, Anna, don't look at me like that, please."

"Like what?"

"Like you don't know whether I'm going to hit you or hug you."

"Well, you weren't exactly happy with me the last time we talked to each other," Anna said with a weak smile.

Nicole smiled back, reaching across the table to squeeze her hand. Anna began to relax. There was the friend she'd known and loved since she was five years old. Somehow they'd sort everything out, it would all be okay. The waiter arrived with chicken Caesar salads for them both, and after he'd gone, Anna gave her friend a good hard look.

"How are you, really?" Anna asked.

Nicole was a little thinner than before, and her face was taut with tension.

"I'm doing okay. Things are…complicated right now."

"You're telling me. Why on earth did you go to work for Nate Hunter? Your father is beside himself."

"Pissed him off, huh?" Nicole said, with her characteristic cheek, before a look of regret shadowed her expressive eyes.

"That's one way of putting it."

"How is he? Someone told me they'd seen him the other day but that he wasn't looking so good. It made me worry about him and it's not like I can just pick up the phone and call him to ask how he is."

"He's doing okay. This whole upset has slowed him down a bit, but—and I'm sure you probably don't want to hear this— Judd is picking up the reins pretty capably."

"Figures. The golden child. Even though I was always there, and he wasn't, I could never measure up to him, you know." Nicole's mouth twisted into a bitter line.

"Your father loves you, Nicole."

"I know, but it's not the same. I could never fill the hole that Judd left, and now he's back."

Anna's heart twisted. She was sure that that wasn't the case. Charles loved both of his children—he'd just gotten in such a habit of being strict with Nicole that he didn't know how to show it. Still, she knew how much it had to hurt to see

Charles lavish the affection on Judd that Nicole had always craved for herself.

"So you won't be coming back to us anytime soon?"

Nicole gave her a haunted look and shook her head. "I...I can't."

"What do you mean, you can't? Of course you can. Your home is with us, your career was with us. Come back, please?"

"No, it's not that simple. Not anymore."

"Why? What is it?"

Nicole shook her head again. "I can't talk about it just now. Maybe later, who knows? I just wanted to see you again and to say sorry for the horrible things I said before. I was upset and I needed someone to blame. Unfortunately, you were it."

"So are we all good now?"

"Yeah, we are. I've missed you so much."

"I've missed you, too."

They finished the rest of their lunch while discussing anything and everything other than work, or men. For some reason Nicole was cagey about the questions Anna started to ask her about Nate Hunter, and Anna certainly wasn't prepared to talk about her feelings for Nicole's brother to her face. It was easier to skirt over those issues and just skim the basics. By the time she had to head back to work, Anna felt so much better for having been able to spend some time with Nicole.

"I'm glad you emailed me," Anna said, standing and giving her friend a hug as their lunch together drew to an end.

"I'm glad you're still talking to me. I don't deserve you, you know."

"Of course you do, and more," Anna replied. "I'll settle the bill, okay? Next time will be your turn."

"Are you sure?"

"That there'll be a next time? Of course there will."

"Not that, silly." Nicole laughed.

Anna felt a sense of relief that she'd finally brought a smile to her friend's face, a smile that, however briefly, dispelled the tension that had been there. She watched Nicole head out the restaurant before she went to the cashier to settle their account. To her surprise, it had already been paid.

"There must be some mistake," she said.

"No, there's no mistake," said an all too familiar voice from behind her. "I figured it was worth the price of lunch to find out what you were up to."

Judd caught her elbow in a firm hold and guided her out the door toward the car park.

"What are you doing here?" she asked, hating the panic in her voice.

"More to the point, what are you doing here?"

"Nicole asked to see me for lunch, that's all."

"All? Seems kind of interesting that the week we lose a considerable amount of business to Jackson Importers you should meet her for lunch. Are you sure you weren't discussing anything else, like the Californian wineries on our list, for example?"

"Of course not! I wouldn't dream of doing anything of the sort." Indignation fueled her to add, "I don't know where you managed to form this incredibly low opinion of me, and I really don't care, but don't keep bringing your insinuations to my face. They are, without exception, wrong."

"So why were you together?"

"We're friends. We've been friends for most of our lives. Did we need a reason?"

"I understood that your friendship was pretty much severed over me."

"Don't rate your effect on people so highly. As I said, we've known each other a very long time. It would take far more than someone like you to destroy that. Look, if you feel that strongly that you can't believe me, why don't you just fire me? In fact, forget that. I quit. I can't work for someone who doesn't even begin to know the meaning of the word *trust*."

Anna pulled her arm free of his hand and headed for her car. She was shaking with anger to think that he could even begin to imagine that she'd do anything to deliberately sabotage Wilson Wines. It would be like slitting her throat, both professionally and personally.

She heard his footfall behind her and she dug in her handbag for her car keys, desperate to get away from him. She wouldn't let him know how much his words today had hurt, just like she hadn't shown him how his belief that she and Charles had been lovers had also cut her.

"Anna, wait!" he called.

But she didn't want to wait. She wanted distance and she wanted it now, before he saw the sheen of tears that now glazed her eyes. Damn it, where were those keys? Long, warm fingers closed over her hand as she finally extracted her keys from the depths of her bag and her finger depressed the remote to unlock her car.

"Anna, stop. I'm sorry. I jumped to conclusions."

"You're pretty good at that, aren't you?" she said bitterly, blinking back the moisture that stung her eyes.

"What can I say, I have a suspicious mind." He smiled back at her, and despite herself she was charmed by his self-deprecating tone. And that was more than half the problem, she acknowledged. He could get under her defenses with no more than a smile.

"I need to get back to the office. Please let me go."

She stared pointedly at his hand, which still captured hers within its warmth.

"Not yet. I want to apologize to you properly. I've been an idiot and I've treated you very unfairly. In my defense I can only say that it started back in Adelaide."

"But surely you can understand why I didn't tell you the truth about why I was there right from the start? For all I knew, you would have just shipped me off the property—which is what you pretty much did anyway after you read the letter."

"I can understand now. And like I said, I am sorry for allowing myself to let that color my judgment about you."

"Fine, I accept your apology. Now let me go."

"Ah, Anna, in such a hurry to leave me?"

He stepped a little closer and Anna felt that all-too familiar thrum of awareness course through her veins. He was like a drug to her, and she was rapidly losing, becoming addicted. She'd let herself become dependent on his kisses, his touch, everything.

"Don't, please."

She dropped her handbag and put up her hand, but he didn't stop moving, not even when her hand became trapped between the wall of his chest and her breasts. He was so close she could see the silver striations that feathered his irises and lent his eyes their particular vivid blue hue. Her heart quickened as she watched his pupils dilate.

"Don't what?" he asked, his voice soft, enticing.

"Don't kiss me."

"Afraid of me, Anna?"

"No," she admitted. "I'm afraid of me."

"I'll keep you safe," he said.

His kiss was short and incredibly sweet. The seal of a promise that offered so very much—perhaps even a chance of a future together that was no longer threatened by the shadows of his family's past. She was trembling when he released her, her entire body screaming for more than just that brief embrace.

Judd bent to collect her bag and handed it to her, then opened her car door, holding it for her as she slid into the driver's seat.

"Will you be okay to get back to the office?"

"Sure," she said, willing her body back under her control.

"I'll see you there."

"Judd? How did you know where to find me?"

He gave a small frown before answering. "There was a page missing from the report you gave me. I went to your computer to reprint it and you'd left your email open."

So for all his apparent mistrust of her, he hadn't been actively snooping. And, he'd *listened* to her—really listened. The thought gave her another little thrill of hope. Anna nodded and pulled her door closed before starting the engine and backing out of the car space. Judd stood to one side, watching her leave. She gave him a small wave and drove out of the car park.

Judd went straight into Anna's office when he arrived back at Wilson Wines.

"About your resignation," he started, closing her office door behind him.

Anna looked up, surprise on her face. "My resignation?"

"Yeah, back at the restaurant. You quit, remember?"

"Ah, yes, so I did."

"Just for the record, I don't accept it."

"For the record," she repeated, a tiny smile on her face, before slowly nodding. "Okay. So we're all good now—I can get back to work?"

"No."

"No? What's wrong?"

"I miss you," he answered simply.

"Miss me? But we see each other every day," she protested.

"Is that enough for you? Really? Tell me, Anna, how are you sleeping at night, knowing I'm just down the hall from you—wanting you as much as you probably want me?"

He watched the muscles in her throat work as she swallowed.

"What? Lost for words?" He moved across the office and

sat in the chair opposite her desk. "Seems to me that we have a pretty good thing between us. Wouldn't you agree?"

"Physically, yes," she finally concurred, although he could see how reluctant she was to admit even that.

"Don't you think we should let that play out? Keep exploring it to its fullest potential?"

To his surprise, sadness seemed to cloud her eyes. Her voice, when she spoke, was flat. "No, I don't. Tell me, Judd, how do you define *potential?*"

Her words surprised him. "Define it? Are you kidding me? You mean you have this level of physical synchronicity with every man you sleep with?"

"And there we have it," Anna said, throwing her hands in the air. "Just how many men do you think I've slept with?"

"Does it matter?"

"No, it doesn't matter, but you continually imply I have loose morals. First you accuse me of sleeping with your father, then you jump to the ridiculous conclusion that I was sharing company information with Nicole." She shook her head emphatically. "There's no way I can even begin to contemplate any kind of relationship with you when you don't trust me at all—over anything!"

"You're right," he admitted, deciding to take another tack on this argument.

He had assumed the worst about her all the way. In the beginning that had partly been her own fault, but he was man enough to admit it had been far easier to remain guarded around her than it was to examine just how much he wanted her, or why. He'd hoped that, as with all his conquests, he'd enjoy the ride while it lasted. After all, he didn't plan to stay in New Zealand forever.

The moment he thought that, though, everything in his mind rebelled. For some reason this had stopped being a temporary fling. He'd gone at this whole exercise looking upon everything as being temporary—expendable even. But somewhere along the line things had changed, and that change started with Anna.

Her voice pulled his attention back. "Of course I'm right. So you'll agree that we should forget about there being any kind of relationship between us, except for at work."

"I can't do that, Anna."

"I beg your pardon?"

"I can't do that. What I can do, if you'll let me, is learn to trust you. To get to know you better and to show you that I'm worth you giving me that chance. Will you at least try with me?"

He watched as her emotions played across her face.

"You want me to try to let *you* trust *me?* You hurt me, Judd—both on a professional level and on a personal one. After we made love down in Nelson and here, in your office—" Her voice hitched and she paused and swallowed before continuing. "Did you honestly think I was so promiscuous as to go from one man's bed to another, and back again?"

"Since we're being honest, I have to admit that it made me furious to think that you could do that."

"But I'm not like that!" Her voice rose in obvious frustration.

"I know that, Anna. I'm learning all the time."

"Fine. Okay, I will try with you. But on one condition."

"What's that?" he asked, knowing the answer before she even verbalized it and hating that, in this at least, he could read her so well.

"I'm not sleeping with you. Not straightaway. We can get to know each other the way normal couples do."

"We've missed a few steps, that's true."

"And I want your word of honor that you won't try to persuade me otherwise. I'm helpless against you. There, I admit it. Show me that I can trust *you.* Don't use that knowledge against me."

Every particle in his body rebelled against the idea, but he found himself nodding in agreement.

"Agreed," he managed, even though his jaw felt tight and his throat barely allowed the single word past it. "A date tonight, then. That'd be a good start. I'll meet you downstairs in the lobby at the house at seven."

What the lady wanted, the lady was definitely going to get. And while it would be a living torment every second until she capitulated to him, he knew that very soon, she'd be his again. And once she was, no matter what his plans for Charles Wilson, he knew she'd stay by *his* side.

Eleven

Anna waited in the lobby at the house and paced the black-and-white-tiled entrance nervously. This was going to be their third date in the three days since last Thursday, when they'd agreed to take things slowly and learn to get to know one another. So far it had been an exercise in pure torture. Judd had been nothing but a complete gentleman. It was driving her crazy.

Today he'd apparently planned a picnic and told her to dress accordingly. Without any idea of what one wore to a picnic these days, she'd opted for a pair of flat navy leather shoes with a peep toe and clear-colored beads embroidered on top, and teamed them up with a pair of three-quarter-length jeans with the cuffs rolled up and a fine-knit pale pink sweater.

Charles came through the lobby.

"Heading out again?" he asked.

"A picnic today, apparently."

He chuckled. "Have to hand it to the boy. He's not only

picked up the business quickly but he hasn't wasted time with you, either. I knew sending you to get him would be a good idea."

A frisson of discomfort spread through her at his words. Had he meant all along for her and Judd to become close? She didn't like the sensation of being manipulated, not even by Charles, who had probably had the greater hand in guiding her life than anyone she knew—even herself. Before she could respond, Judd came down the stairs.

Dressed in jeans and a silver-gray long-sleeved turtleneck, he looked good enough to eat. Anna blinked and turned her head away. She shouldn't be thinking about him along those lines. He'd adhered to her dictates about their dating to the letter. It was contrary of her to wish now that he hadn't.

"All ready, that's good."

Judd flung her a smile that lent his eyes a wicked gleam. He was up to something, she just knew it. Every cell in her body responded to him as he drew closer and put an arm around her shoulders.

"We'll probably be out for most of the day. Will you be okay?" he asked his father.

"Sure, I'm fine. There's always someone around here if I need something." Charles waved his inquiry away.

Anna looked at the older man sharply. His color wasn't good today and there was an air of frailty about him that sent a ripple of concern through her.

"Are you feeling all right today?" she asked. "We can postpone our outing, it's no bother."

"Anna, I've said it before and I'll say it again. Stop your fussing. I'm big enough and old enough to look after myself. Now off you go and have a great day. Don't you worry about me."

"You heard the man," Judd said, steering her toward the front doors. "Besides," he reminded her when they were out of Charles's earshot, "the household staff has our cell numbers. I've already talked to them about calling me if he seems like he needs help."

"So you agree with me, then. He's not looking so good this week, is he?"

"I've noticed. At the beginning of the week I tried to talk to him about cutting his hours down, but he's nothing if not stubborn."

"A family trait, no doubt," Anna commented.

Judd's lips quirked in response. "No doubt," he agreed.

They went out the front doors of the house and down the stairs to the driveway. Anna looked around but there was no sign of a car.

"Are we walking? Maybe I should change my shoes."

"No, don't change a thing. You're perfect as you are. We need to go to the tennis courts."

"Tennis? Then I definitely need to change my shoes."

"No, we won't be playing tennis," Judd answered.

Totally puzzled, Anna walked alongside him. As she did, she became aware of the air-beating sound of rotors coming toward them. A helicopter? Sure enough, a sleek black chopper was coming toward them, stirring up the air and the early-falling leaves as it lowered onto the tennis courts at the end of the property.

Anna turned and looked at Judd. "You said we were going for a picnic."

"And we are. Just not locally."

He shepherded her to the helicopter and opened the rear door, handing her up into one of the seats and passing a head-set to her before following her up and settling in next to her. Anna felt her stomach lurch as the chopper slowly lifted off and circled the property before heading out toward the harbor.

"Did I mention that I don't like small aircraft to you?" she asked, her knuckles white as she gripped the edges of her seat.

Judd's hand pried one of hers free from its hold. "I remember, but I was hoping that perhaps I could distract you on this trip."

He lifted her hand to his mouth and kissed her palm. The instant his lips touched her she felt the familiar tug of desire swell through her body. Oh, yes, he could distract her that way, all right. She hazarded a look out the window as Judd stroked the soft inner skin of her wrist, then dragged her eyes back to him again. His clear gaze met hers.

"Trust me, Anna. I won't let anything hurt you."

She nodded and swallowed, his voice soft and gentle as it filled her ears from within the cups of her headphones. He kept up a steady stream of soothing words, and she'd lost track of how long they'd been in the air when the helicopter began to descend and her stomach lurched again. Judd's fingers closed around hers reassuringly.

"You're doing great," he said. "Anyone would think you're an old hand at this."

"I doubt that, but thanks," she managed, feeling a surge of relief as the skids touched down on terra firma. Judd opened his door and hopped down before turning to help Anna out.

"Keep your head and arms down," he warned.

No problem, she thought as the wind whipped her hair around her face. She ducked down and let Judd lead her toward a glass-fronted building not far from where they'd landed. Behind them, the helicopter took off and wheeled away back over the water.

"He is coming back for us, right?" she asked.

Judd laughed, the sound curling around her heart and squeezing it tight. She felt a momentary panic. When did he start meaning so much to her?

"Of course, all in good time."

"Where are we?" Anna asked, looking around her. As far as she could tell, the dwelling ahead of them was the only one to be seen and there were no boats moored at the small bay in front of them.

"Near Kawau Island. I heard about this place and thought we'd enjoy the solitude. Come on, let's go and see what's on the menu."

Anna followed him up to the building and inside, where a spacious lounge/dining area flowed into a well-equipped kitchen. As Anna walked around to get the lay of the land, a small but luxurious bathroom with floor-length clear-glass windows facing back into native bush behind the building surprised her, while another room, a bedroom, saw her closing the door on it quickly. She didn't want to think about that. Not when they were just starting to get to know one another.

In the kitchen, Judd had removed a bottle of chilled champagne from the refrigerator as well as a platter of antipasto.

"Let's take this outside," he suggested. "Grab the glasses, will you?"

Anna reached for a pair of champagne flutes from a shelf over the kitchen sink and followed Judd out onto the wide deck that faced the bay.

"This is beautiful," she said, sitting down next to Judd on the simple wooden steps that led down off the deck and onto a well-kept lawn. "It's like a world within a world."

Judd reached up and smoothed a strand of hair from her cheeks. "It's a great place to get to know one another better, without everything else intruding."

He deftly dealt with the foil and the cage on the bottle before pouring them each a foaming glass of the golden sparkling liquid.

"Mmm, French," Anna commented, sighting the label and then taking a sip. "Oh, yes, there's nothing quite like it."

Judd didn't comment, and her eyes flew to his in the silence that stretched out between them. He was watching her, his gaze intent, the pupils dilated, his lips parted as if he'd been about to say something but the words had fled before they could be uttered. He blinked, breaking the spell that had locked them together all too briefly, and lifted his glass to his lips.

"I agree," he said, putting his glass down and reaching for a stuffed olive on the platter. "The French definitely have a knack for it."

They fell silent for a while, enjoying the wine, the food, the setting, but then Anna turned to Judd to ask, "Do you remember much of your time with your father, before you went to Australia?"

He sighed and for a moment she wondered if she'd trod on some very sensitive memories.

"I remember quite a bit. I was six when we left. I remember him always being larger than life. Always busy, always entertaining, always booming with noise. I couldn't wait for the moment he stepped in the door at the end of a day, and when he was away on business I'd mark every day off on the calendar until he returned. Despite the fact he was constantly busy with work and clients, he always made time for me."

"It must have been hard when you left."

"Hard?" He laughed but the sound held no joy to it. "I was devastated. My mother was angry and hurt, and no one in Australia had a good word to say about him. It was like my life had turned upside down overnight. I had quite a few issues with his abandonment of me—of both of us."

"No wonder you weren't keen to reestablish a relationship with him."

"No, I wasn't. Despite the fact that I know there are two sides to every story, I find it very hard to understand, or forgive, the way he just cut me from his life like that."

Judd's dark brows drew together, lending a fierce cast to his features.

"But he's reached out to you now. You're here, you're working with him. You must have forgiven him."

The expression on Judd's face cleared. "Yes, I am working with him now."

There was something in the tone of his voice that struck a chord of concern deep inside. It occurred to her that he hadn't agreed that he had forgiven his father. Before she could say anything more, he flashed a smile at her and rose to his feet, putting out a hand.

"Come on, let's go for a wander along the shoreline."

Anna put her hand in his and pushed her worries aside. She was probably being oversensitive, a state she was becoming used to around Judd Wilson.

When they returned from the beach, they went inside to gather together the rest of the lunch fixings that had been left in the fridge for them. Judd poured them each another glass of champagne outside on the deck, while Anna made up plates of slices of fresh-baked ciabatta together with ripe wedges of Camembert and slivers of prosciutto. She added a few slices of sun-dried tomato from the leftover antipasto to the open sandwich she'd put together on her plate and lifted it to her mouth to take a bite.

"Oh, my, that's good," she said after she'd chewed and swallowed the mouthful.

"It looks delicious," Judd agreed. "Mind if I have a taste?"

"Sure," she said, offering him her sandwich.

He ignored the offering in her hand, instead leaning over their dishes, and licked the lower edge of her bottom lip. She saw a tiny piece of cheese on the tip of his tongue before he swallowed it.

"Oh, yes, just how I like it. Ripe and soft. Warm and ready to eat."

A heated flush spread through her, a flush that made every nerve ending stand on end. It had been her call to keep the physical side of their discovery of one another out of the equation. A call he'd respected to a degree that had slowly begun to drive her crazy. Crazy for him.

"Would you like some more?" she managed to say, not taking her eyes from his.

"Sure," he answered.

She picked up a small wedge of the cheese between a thumb and forefinger and held it up to his mouth. His lips closed around the morsel, his tongue abrading her fingers as he did so and sending a shudder of longing straight to the pit of her belly. A familiar tingling started low down in her body and spread out to her extremities.

"More?" she asked.

Instead of answering, he reached out to cup one hand behind her head and gently drew her to him.

"More of you," he said simply before his mouth took hers.

His lips were gentle, coaxing, and she felt herself melt into him. She heard the clatter of dishes as he swept them to one side before hooking his arm around her waist and sliding her closer to him. Suddenly she couldn't be close enough. Her arms lifted and hooked around his neck, her breasts pressed up against his chest—and still she wasn't close enough.

She pulled her lips away.

"Um, Judd? About that condition I made? About us not…"

"Uh-huh," he said, nuzzling her neck.

"I was reacting under duress. I—"

"Anna?"

"Mmm?"

"Shut up and kiss me again."

So she did. Judd lifted her up and guided her to straddle his lap, shoving his hands up under her top and across her back. His hands were hot against her skin and she wanted to feel more of him. She reached for the hem of his sweater, pulling it up and exposing his belly and chest before grazing her nails across his muscled torso. Beneath her fingertips she felt the disks of his nipples grow firm and rigid and she gently pushed him back down onto the wooden deck. As she did so, Judd eased the turtleneck off, leaving his upper body completely bare to her touch.

She bent down and placed a kiss in the hollow at the base

of his throat before tracing her tongue across his collarbone. Every now and then she paused to nip at his skin. He felt so fine, tasted so good, she wanted to savor every second she had with him at her mercy. Her fingers traced the muscles that corded his rib cage, feeling his skin react under her feather-fine touch, and she smiled against his skin as she traced ever-decreasing circles with her tongue around his nipples.

Her hands worked their way lower, slowly unbuckling his belt and unbuttoning his jeans before easing inside the now-constricted fabric. She rubbed one hand along the length of his powerful erection, back and forth through the fabric of his briefs, her lips slowly following the path of her hands until her breath warmed his skin at his waistband. She tugged at his jeans and he lifted his hips slightly, allowing her to slide the fabric down to his thighs and tug down the elasticized band of his briefs, exposing the tip of his arousal to her gaze. A tiny bead of moisture gathered at the swollen dark tip of him and she bent her head, tasting it with the very tip of her tongue.

Oh, yes, he tasted so very good. She closed her lips around him, rasping her tongue around his tender flesh again and again before she drew him deeper into her mouth. Judd's fingers pushed through her hair, cupping her head and holding her against him. Not so firmly that she couldn't withdraw if she wanted to, but encouraging her to continue her assault on that most sensitive and responsive part of him.

Anna curled the fingers of one hand around the base of his shaft and moved them firmly up, then down again, all the time taking him deeper into her mouth while stroking her tongue along him with ever-increasing pressure. She felt him begin to shake beneath her and increased the speed of her movements, one hand still stroking him, the other clutching at the bunched fabric of his jeans. A groan tore from his throat as he began to come, and she took it all with a sense of power that vied with her own arousal to see him so undone beneath her ministrations. She might be helpless in the face of her desire for him, but he was equally so for her, she realized, and the knowledge gave her a sense of control and power she'd never known before.

Spent, Judd relaxed back on the deck, his fingers still tangled in her hair as she slowly released him, first with her hand, then with her mouth. She slid up his body, peppering the surface with tiny kisses all the way, swirling her tongue inside the indent of his belly button—the action making his penis twitch in response against her.

She rolled to his side, letting the fingers of one hand stroke softly over his belly and chest as his breathing slowly returned to normal.

"When you change your mind, you really change your mind, don't you?" he said.

"I like to do things thoroughly, or not at all," she replied in kind.

"Then you won't object if we go inside, where we can *thoroughly* explore the aspects available to us?"

In reply, Anna rose to her feet and held out a hand to Judd's supine form. He took her hand and levered himself up, straightening his briefs and yanking his jeans up to his hips, but leaving them undone. She had never seen anything so sexy before as the man standing in front of her. His hair was mussed, his eyes still glowing with the residual pleasure she'd given him. And his body—he was muscled but not heavily, strong but not overpowering. And he was looking at her like she was the only woman in the world. He was everything she'd ever dreamed of, and more. Judd lifted up the champagne bottle and their glasses, and together they walked back into the cottage.

He hadn't been kidding about being thorough. By the time the helicopter returned for them, it was dark and Anna had never felt more sated on every level. Together they'd made love, eaten, bathed, made love and eaten again. If she could ever repeat a day in her life over and again, it would be this one and it was with this thought that Anna acknowledged the truth of her feelings. She was in love with Judd Wilson.

Twelve

Judd woke to a Monday morning heralded by rain and gusting winds. The flip side of autumn had arrived, and with it Anna had capitulated. Last night she'd come to him, breaking what she had insisted was her hard-and-fast rule about respecting Charles and refusing to sleep with Judd under his father's roof. Strangely, he hadn't felt the smug satisfaction he'd expected when he'd felt her slip naked in between the sheets of his bed.

Something had changed during the day while they'd been alone together. Something that made her body curving around his, within the expanse of his bed, the most natural thing in the world. Something he didn't want to deal with. Later would be soon enough, he decided, as he rolled out of the covers and padded on bare feet across the thick carpet toward his en suite bathroom.

By the time he'd completed his shower, Anna had left his bed, and when he got downstairs to the breakfast room she was already there, looking her usual serene and unruffled self and talking to Charles. No one would have dreamed she was such a vixen in bed.

"Good morning," he said with a smile.

To his delight, she blushed. "Good morning to you, too."

"Sleep well?"

He couldn't resist provoking her. He, better than anyone, knew how well she had slept in those tiny snatches when they were both so exhausted they finally left one another well alone.

"Thank you, I did," she replied before lifting her morning coffee to her lips.

Lips that had done wild things to him yesterday. He slammed the door on his wayward thoughts. There was a time and a place for everything. For now he needed to concentrate on Wilson Wines. He felt like he'd reached a crossroads in relation to the business. While he'd come here with the express intent of undermining everything his father had worked for, and delivering his share of the business on a platter to his father's strongest competitor, there was a part of him now that hesitated.

Growing Wilson Wines in a new direction excited him, but did he really want to throw away the revenge he'd longed for ever since he'd accepted his father would never come to get him? It was a difficult decision, and one he would have to face soon.

As an added factor, his mother had started to email him regularly, asking for updates on the house and pestering him to allow her to visit. Right now, Cynthia was the last complication he needed. Her bitterness toward Charles had only grown over the years, and the prospect of seeing the two of them under one roof again was enough to make the milk in his cereal curdle.

He shot a look across the table at Charles. The older man looked gray and tired. Judd had no doubt that following through on his initial plans would see his father into an early

grave and that thought clenched tight in his chest. Somewhere along the line, he'd developed respect for Charles and
particularly for his business acumen. He'd held it together
through stock market crashes, recession and more. Wilson
Wines, while not reaching its fullest potential, was still doing
extremely well in what had been a difficult and competitive
market.

Judd still bore a grudge over the way Charles had handled
his personal life, and the way he had treated his wife and son,
but he felt a little more sympathy now. He'd seen how deeply
angry and hurt Charles could be at what he perceived as disloyalty from someone he loved. Even though he'd jumped to
conclusions and judged unfairly, the suspicion that Cynthia
had been cheating on him must have hit him hard.

Additionally, the challenges for Charles of running a
company—by himself, since the split with his business partner had happened around then, hadn't it?—and dealing with
a marriage that had been falling apart must have taken its toll
on his behavior. And according to Anna, Charles was already
struggling with diabetes-related health issues then, which
couldn't have helped. None of that justified his actions, but
taking everything into account did help to put them in per-
spective.

He looked again at Charles, watched as he picked up his
knife to butter a slice of toast and saw the way his hand
trembled, then looked away as a sharp spear of concern shot
through him. He didn't want his father's further deterioration
to be on his hands.

A loud clatter of cutlery on a plate, followed by Anna's
gasp of shock, dragged his attention back to Charles, who
now leaned to one side in his chair, his color even worse than
before, his eyes closed and his breathing laboring in his chest.

"Quick," he said to Anna, "call an ambulance."

Anna raced out the room and Judd shot to his father's
side, loosening his tie and the top button of his shirt before

lowering Charles to the floor. Charles's skin was cool and clammy to the touch, and Judd felt a surge of genuine fear pour through him.

Charles slipped in and out of consciousness, oblivious to Judd's voice as he repeatedly fired questions at him in an effort to keep his father awake. By the time the ambulance arrived, Judd was beginning to worry that the older man wouldn't make it.

As Anna gave the paramedics a rundown of Charles's health and medications, he began to understand just how fragile his father's life was.

"I'll go with him in the ambulance," Judd said as Charles was lifted onto a gurney and carted out toward the waiting vehicle.

Anna nodded and squeezed his hand. "I'll see you at the hospital. I'll just need to make a few calls first. Let people know we won't be in to the office."

"Thanks."

Judd followed the medics out to the ambulance and was directed into a passenger seat in the front of the vehicle. The ride to Auckland City Hospital was short, although for Judd it felt as if it took hours. Craning his head to see in the back, he watched as the ambulance officer attended to his father and took stats, which he then radioed ahead to the hospital emergency room. Seeing Charles so helpless made the seriousness of his father's state really hit home.

At the hospital there was a blur of activity, and Judd was forced to wait as a medical team took over his father's assessment and treatment. Finally Anna arrived, her face pale and concerned but lightening a little when she saw him. The instant they made eye contact, Judd began to feel some of the tension within him unwind just a notch and he took Anna into his arms, relishing the feel of her and soaking up the comfort her embrace provided.

"How's he doing?" Anna said as she pulled away.

"They're still doing tests."

A sudden flurry of activity at the emergency room door dragged his attention in that direction and he saw his sister striding through the door.

"Where is he? I want to see him."

Anna interceded before he could speak.

"He's with the doctors. They're still assessing him."

"What happened?" Nicole demanded, turning to Judd, her eyes snapping fire.

"He collapsed at breakfast," Judd replied.

"I thought your being here was supposed to make him feel better, not worse," Nicole fired back before promptly bursting into tears.

Judd bit back the response that flew to his tongue, that perhaps if his sister hadn't left the way she did, Charles wouldn't have been pushing himself so hard with work when he should have been taking things easier. But he could see Nicole was fighting her own demons.

A nurse came toward them. "Mr. Wilson, you can see your father now."

Judd reached for Anna, who shook her head. "No, take Nicole. She needs to be with him more than I do."

With a shrug, Judd turned to Nicole. "Are you coming?"

"Of course I'm coming. He's *my* father."

Together they followed the nurse. Charles was conscious but still looked terribly ill. Lines ran into his arms and monitors were beeping around him.

"What's she doing here?" he rasped, staring at Nicole with a mixture of surprise and anger.

Judd felt his sister stiffen at his side.

"I came to see if you were all right, but obviously you're just fine. You won't be needing me here," she said with a quiet dignity that didn't quite mask the hurt in her eyes.

Judd watched her walk back the way she'd come. Anna

went to intercept her but was brushed away as Nicole kept walking straight toward the exit.

"Was that really necessary?" Judd asked his father, going to stand next to his bed.

"She betrayed us. She made the decision to leave us—that means that this isn't her place any longer, here with us. You'd do well to remember that, my boy." The strain of forcing the words he'd had to say took its toll, and Charles's eyes slid closed again.

A bitter taste flooded Judd's mouth. Betrayed, yes, like his father had betrayed the love and trust of his only son by sending him away—banishing him with his mother to another country. Judd couldn't believe that only an hour ago, he'd been halfway convinced he should forgive his father's actions. The man didn't deserve Judd's compassion, or his forgiveness. Look at how he'd just treated his daughter—banishing her with the same ease he'd banished Judd and his mother so long ago. The concern he'd felt for his father diminished as it was replaced by the old familiar anger, and with it, his resolve to continue on his original course hardened.

Anna straightened up the last of the paperwork she'd been collating and put it in her briefcase, ready to bring home and discuss with Judd this evening. She and Judd took turns at the hospital during the allocated visiting times—today was his turn while she covered at the office.

Charles had slipped into a coma after his admission and things had been touch-and-go over the past five days. If he recovered, it was clear that dialysis would be a regular part of his life from here on in. There was no word yet on when he would be allowed back home, but Anna had already made inquiries with private nursing bureaus to ensure he had the care he would need when, God willing, that eventually happened.

While Judd went through the motions of visiting with his father, Anna was certain there was a new distance now between son and father. Something had happened on the day Charles was admitted to hospital, which had created an intangible wall between them. Judd wouldn't be drawn on the subject and Nicole had also retreated back behind her curtain of silence. Well, there was nothing for it but to be there if they needed her, Anna had decided and, as far as Judd was concerned, being where she was needed meant that she was in his bed at night and by his side during the day.

Rain swiped at her windscreen as she drove home. It was already dark and she was bone weary as she pulled her car into the multicar garage at the back of the house. What she needed most right now was a long, relaxing soak in the bath, followed by dinner and maybe a good movie. She wondered if Judd would be up for that, too. A bath together would be just the distraction they both deserved after the past working week. She already could feel herself relaxing by increments as she imagined it.

Anna felt the difference in the house the moment she set foot inside. It wasn't anything she could immediately put her finger on, but something had changed and it **was** more than the fact that the hall flowers were arranged on the left-hand side of the hall table, rather than the middle where they normally stood.

She made her way to the front of the house and the main stairs but her feet arrested on the tiled surface of the lobby as a vaguely familiar voice greeted her from halfway up the stairs.

"I should have known you'd be living here," Cynthia drawled with an expression of distaste on her elegant features.

"Cynthia? I didn't know you were coming," Anna managed through lips that felt stiff with shock.

"I'm sure Judd doesn't find it necessary to tell you *everything,* my dear," Cynthia replied as she continued down the stairs and came to a halt one step up from the bottom—a position that continued to force Anna to look up at her.

"I trust Mrs. Evans has made you comfortable."

"Mrs. Evans? Oh, yes, that housekeeper. She'll have to go when I'm back here permanently, you know. No idea of etiquette whatsoever."

"What do you mean, when you're here permanently?"

"When my ex-husband dies, of course. I came as soon as I heard he was ill. So sad for you all, but only to be expected."

"Charles is improving every day. I don't know where you got the idea that he's dying," Anna replied staunchly. "And I'm not that certain he would like you under his roof."

"I think you're forgetting a vitally important point," Cynthia said with a smile that was as cold as the expression in her eyes.

"And what would that be?" Anna asked, feeling the hairs on the back of her neck rise in response to the woman's attitude.

"That this is Judd's house now and, very soon, he'll be giving it to me."

With that, Cynthia swept past Anna in the direction of the salon. All thoughts of a relaxing bath now banished from her mind, Anna went upstairs to her room to change and try and clear her head. Of course the house was now Judd's. How could she have forgotten that? Had he planned to install his mother back in here all along? And what of Charles? What would happen to him when he was well enough to come out of the hospital?

She rushed through a shower and changed into a more comfortable pair of wide-legged black trousers and a long-sleeved tunic top, also in black but chased with silver threads that broke the starkness of the garment. Once she was dressed and had reapplied her makeup, she felt better able to cope with the perfectly coiffed woman who was downstairs. During her shower she'd all but talked herself into believing that Cynthia was sadly mistaken and that Judd transferring the property into her name was a possibility so remote it was laughable.

But a tightening low down in her gut told her it was entirely possible. The doubts that she'd had for the past few days surged up to remind her of what Judd had told her about his mother's obsession with Masters' Rise.

Anna drew in a deep breath and tried to summon the courage she knew she'd need to face Cynthia downstairs. No, it was no good. No amount of breathing would make her feel right about this. She'd just have to haul on her big-girl panties and get it over with. She descended the stairs with a knot in her stomach the size of a boulder, and headed for the salon. Inside, Cynthia sat upon one of the love seats, a glass of wine in her hand and a disapproving look upon her face.

"I'll need to do quite a bit of upgrading," she commented. "Charles has really let this place slide."

Anna felt her back stiffen in response. Not only had Charles done everything *but* let the place slide, Anna's mother had enjoyed a free hand in redecorating and refurbishing as and when required.

"It's a home," Anna answered carefully. "Charles felt it was important that we be comfortable."

"Well, you've certainly been comfortable here, haven't you? I imagine it was quite the come up in ranks from where you and your mother used to live. Tell me, how is dear Donna these days?"

"My mother passed away several years ago," Anna responded uncomfortably. She'd bet Cynthia never called Donna Garrick "dear" anything to her face the whole time she'd known her.

"I am sorry to hear that." Cynthia took a sip of her wine before continuing, "And yet, you're still here. Why is that?"

"Charles said it was to be my home for as long as I wanted."

"But it's no longer his place to offer you that roof over your head." Cynthia shook her head, an expression of sympathy on her face that looked as false as the tone of her voice. "I'd suggest you begin looking elsewhere for your accommodation, although I doubt you'll be as lucky as to find anyone as...*accommodating* as Charles."

"I really don't think it's quite your place to suggest where I should be living," Anna snapped back, suddenly angry where before she'd only felt apprehension. "Judd wouldn't dream of putting me out from under his roof."

"Ah, so the kitten has claws. How charming." Cynthia laughed—the sound grating along Anna's last nerve. "Although you may not feel quite so inclined to leap to Judd's defense when you understand what Judd's plan was all along. Ask yourself, with everything he has in Adelaide, why else would he have come back if not for some well-aimed revenge? It's not as if Charles was ever a father to him.

"You look shocked. Poor dear, I suppose Judd has taken you to his bed and now you've gone and fallen in love with him." Cynthia shook her head and tsked softly. "He's only using you, you know. Despite everything, Judd's a lot like Charles. He won't marry you. Do you really think you're worthy of a place like this when your mother never was? Like father like son, like mother like daughter. My son will ask you to leave soon enough. Wouldn't you rather save face and go before that happens?"

Anna reeled under the onslaught of Cynthia's words. "Judd wouldn't do that," she said woodenly.

Or would he? Her fingers curled in her palms, her nails biting into the skin—the pain an offset to the pain that now squeezed her heart tight. She really didn't know Judd Wilson beyond what he'd presented to her. She knew he was determined and had an edge of ruthlessness lingering beneath the surface at all times. Could Cynthia's words be the truth? She didn't want to believe it. She loved him. He wasn't that kind of man.

Anna felt an arctic chill shiver through her body. Despite her instinct to protest Cynthia's words, they held all too much of a ring of truth about them. The older woman had given voice to Anna's greatest fear—that she would never have the wholehearted love of the man she loved in return.

Thirteen

Judd was exhausted as he got out of his car and climbed the front steps into the house. Funny how it had so rapidly begun to feel like home, he realized, when before it had always been nothing more than something to be acquired and used. Perhaps it was the thought of the woman waiting inside for him. He knew Anna had already left the office and would be waiting for his report on Charles's condition.

He felt like a hypocrite attending the old man at the hospital, but today hadn't been a good one for his father, with his health deteriorating further. Even unconscious, Charles didn't make a good patient. In fact, Judd suspected the word "patient" was totally lacking in his vocabulary. Still, he'd seemed more settled when Judd had left him.

It had been a tough day all around, really. He'd battled with his decision to go ahead and test the waters with Nate Hunter but, in the face of Charles's treatment of Nicole at the hospital, eventually he'd decided to go ahead. He'd spent the better part of the morning trying to set up a meeting with

Hunter, but the man was as elusive as quicksilver. Judd hadn't wanted to leave a message with Nate's staff—all too aware that Nicole could easily intercept it and somehow block him reaching the other man altogether. Maybe tomorrow would see success.

Judd considered the paperwork inside his briefcase. He hadn't dared to leave it in the office in case Anna saw it before he'd completed his plans. Everything had to be lined up just so for all this to work. She wouldn't be happy, and he hoped their burgeoning relationship would weather the fallout once it all went ahead. Her place was with him now; surely she'd see he had no other choice.

He waited for the sense of satisfaction that usually infused him when he thought of his plans coming to fruition, but instead he felt oddly flat. Must just be tired, he rationalized. Between nights with Anna, demanding days in the office and even more demanding time at the hospital, he was definitely not operating at his peak.

As he entered the front lobby he could hear women's voices from the salon. He dropped his briefcase near a hall table and walked through, gritting his teeth as he tried to force a welcoming smile onto his face. The last thing he felt up to right now was company, but appearances had to be maintained.

He could barely believe his eyes as he pushed open the salon door.

"Mother?"

Cynthia rose from her seat and put out her arms to her son. Automatically, Judd crossed the room and allowed his mother to embrace him.

"My boy, I've missed you."

"Why are you here?"

Cynthia pouted. "What? Didn't you miss me, too?"

"Of course," Judd said, brushing her words aside.

She was the last person he wanted to deal with right now.

His plans for Wilson Wines needed to be carefully executed and he didn't need the distraction of worrying if his mother was about to preempt his weeks of carefully layered construction—or *de*construction as the case would be.

He cast a look in Anna's direction. She was pale and sitting with her spine rigid. Her hazel eyes were clouded with an emotion he couldn't quite put his finger on. His protective instincts rose to the surface—surprising him with their intensity. Anna had been fine when he'd spoken to her at the office before he'd headed off to the hospital, which meant that whatever had upset her had happened between then and now. That only left one person who was likely to be the cause, which begged the question, what had Cynthia done to upset Anna?

"Everything okay at the office?" he asked.

"Of course," Anna replied. "I have some papers in my case for you when you have a moment."

"Surely you two can leave work alone for one evening. I've just arrived and I want to hear everything about what you've been up to while you've been gone," Cynthia interjected.

"Let me leave you two to it," Anna said, rising coolly from her seat. "I have plenty to attend to while you catch up."

"You don't need to go," Judd said, wondering why Anna seemed so keen to create some distance between them.

"Let her," his mother said, her long fingers tightening around his forearm. "It'll be lovely to be just the two of us over dinner, don't you think?"

He didn't think anything of the kind. Something was terribly wrong and he had no idea what it was.

"I'll speak to you later, then. If you're sure you won't join us?"

A crooked smile twisted Anna's lips. "Oh, I'm sure. You two enjoy catching up. I'll leave the papers in your room."

He watched with narrowed eyes as Anna left the room, closing the salon door with silent precision. Something was very wrong and the minute she'd gone he felt the exhaustion of earlier tug at him again.

"I wish you'd told me you were coming to visit," Judd said to his mother as they assumed their seats.

"I was hoping to surprise you."

Judd felt a flare of anger burst inside. Surprise him? She had to be kidding. When everything hung so carefully in the balance it was the last thing he needed.

"You certainly succeeded at that," he said ruefully. "How long are you planning to stay?"

"A week, maybe," Cynthia replied. "Longer, if necessary."

"Longer?" The word slipped out before he could prevent it. He was more tired than he thought.

"What's the matter, Judd? You know what we planned."

"Yes, and I also know you were supposed to wait until I told you to come over."

"But I heard that your father was gravely ill—not from you, I might add."

"He's ill, Mother, not dead."

"Well, either way," Cynthia said airily, her hands fluttering in the air, "if you want him to be aware of your revenge, then you're running out of time. You've got to get to work on taking it all over and doing with it what you want to—which is to give the house to me, right?"

That was what they'd planned, but Judd felt himself reluctant to commit to agreeing with her. The whole time he'd grown up at The Masters' he'd always felt as though he didn't fully belong. Strangely enough, he felt as if he fitted here.

He redirected his mother's conversation to the family back at The Masters' as they went through to dinner, but all the while he was acutely conscious of Anna's empty chair at the table. When he was finished with his meal he excused himself, citing business he urgently needed to attend to, and he went back to the lobby to retrieve his briefcase.

He was surprised to see a stack of suitcases by the front

door. They hadn't been there when he'd arrived home, and they couldn't be his mother's. She would have complained long and hard if the airline had lost her luggage, however temporarily. A sound on the staircase behind him made him turn to see Anna, an overnight bag in one hand and her handbag slung over one shoulder.

"What's this?" he demanded, his hand flung out toward the cases at his feet.

Outside, he heard a car pull up on the driveway and give a toot.

"My stuff. I'm moving out. That'll be Mr. Evans with my car." She stepped past him to open the front door and hefted one of her cases onto the front porch. "Thanks for bringing my car around. I hope we can fit everything in," she said to the handyman as he came up the stairs to get her cases.

"What do you mean, you're moving out?"

"Just that." She turned to Evans and gestured to the rest of her things in the lobby. "All of these, too, please."

"Hold on a minute. Where are you going and, more important, why?"

Anna shook her head. "I think you know why. Tell me, did you really come back to wreak revenge on your father? Did you mean to give this house to your mother all along?"

He stood in silence. A silence that damned him in her eyes. Eyes that were now hazed with pain and a sorrow that went so deep he wanted to do anything and everything to make it go away.

Her voice was hoarse when she spoke. "You always thought the worst of me, but it never occurred to me to think you were capable of something like this. I didn't want to believe you could be so calculating, but it seems I was terribly wrong. I really don't know you at all, do I?"

Evans had collected the last of her bags and was now waiting by her car. Anna started to head out the door. Judd wanted to call out to her, to physically restrain her from leaving, but he knew he had no right. He *had* meant to give his mother this house all along and he had meant so much more harm to Charles, as well. Right now, though, none of that seemed important anymore as the woman he suddenly realized had come to mean so much to him walked out the door.

A slow burn of anger started deep inside of him. He had never lost control of a situation ever before, and right now everything he'd worked hard for these past weeks, his whole lifetime, in fact, started to crumble. He rubbed at his eyes, unable to dislodge the picture of the misery on Anna's face no matter how hard he tried.

"It's for the best, Judd." His mother's voice came from behind him and he whirled around to face her.

"For the best? What makes you say that?"

"She had ideas above her station and she'd have eventually dragged you down to her level. You know that, don't you? After all, look at what her mother did for Charles. Nothing. She was a convenient mistress and a passable housekeeper. No doubt Anna's been riding on her mother's abilities to sneak her way into Charles's wealth through his bed, too." Cynthia stepped closer, placing one hand on his arm and closing her fingers around it in a hold that surprised him with its strength. "Trust me, Judd. You're better off without her."

He stared at his mother's fingers and their clawlike grip, the physical manifestation of her hold on him the perfect analogy for how she'd tried to direct him all his life. As her words ran through his mind—words that he knew, in this case, to be totally untrue—he wondered what else his mother had told him that had been twisted and distorted away from the truth to suit her own manipulations.

"Did you tell her?"

"About the house? Of course I did. She needed to know, Judd. She doesn't belong here any more than her mother ever did."

"She was an *invited* guest under this roof."

His mother's face paled beneath expertly applied cosmetics. "I don't like your implication, Judd."

"Like it or not, it's still my name on the deed to this property."

"A mere technicality. You know what this place means to me."

"More than anything or anyone else, yes."

Weariness swamped him with the awareness that Cynthia's obsession with this property was outside normal perceptions. Clearly she felt it was owed to her for all she'd lost when she was younger, and for all she'd endured during her marriage to Charles and her subsequent banishment back home to Australia. It was unhealthy and Judd was annoyed with himself that he'd never seen it before now.

Cynthia was Cynthia. She'd never pretended to be anything else but what she'd presented to the world. Subterfuge had never been her style, ever, which was why he'd always assumed that she'd never been anything but honest with him. Only now did he realize that while she didn't lie, per se, her accounts on matters that affected her deeply were twisted by her bitterness into something that only vaguely resembled the truth. Accepting that, and the fact that as an adult he should have seen it sooner, filled him with a fury at himself that he could barely contain.

She'd always be his mother, and he'd always love her as such, but right now he didn't like the person she was very much at all. He needed some distance between them before his anger bubbled over and he said something he might regret.

All his instincts urged him to follow Anna, but with that he was forced to admit he had no idea where to go to look for her. Frustration rose within him anew. Even if he did know where to find her, he doubted she was in the mood to listen to him. He pulled himself free of his mother's clasp, the movement as metaphorical as it was literal.

"Look, it's late and I have work to get through. I'll see you in the morning and we can discuss your return to The Masters'."

"My return? But I've only just arr—"

"We'll talk in the morning," he said firmly, and grabbing his briefcase he went upstairs.

Anna didn't know how much longer she could take this. Working with Judd and feeling about him the way she did, yet knowing just how ruthless he really was, was making her feel sick inside. She had hardly slept over the weekend. The cheap motel she'd discovered on Friday night was hardly in a secluded area and the constant traffic noise and the racket from a nearby bar and club had ensured her nights were punctuated by the kinds of sounds that had dragged her from her restless sleep with a start more than once.

When she'd left the house on Friday she'd been too distraught to think carefully about where she was headed. In the end, to avoid creating an accident, she'd pulled into the motel thinking that it would be for only a night before she found an apartment in the city. But the weekend had passed in a blur of visits to the hospital, timing them to avoid Judd, and spending the rest of her time wallowing in a blend of self-pity and self-disgust that she could have been so foolish as to lose her heart to a man as cold and unforgiving as Judd Wilson.

After a lifetime of promising herself she deserved so much more than her mother had settled for, she'd just gone and found herself falling into the same pattern. Falling in love with a man with whom she would never be an equal—a man who would never offer her more than a job and his bed to sleep in.

She wished she could turn her feelings off as easily as Judd had appeared to do. He'd come into the office this Monday morning with nothing but a professional attitude and a driving work ethic. She should be grateful for that, at least, she thought as she brought his mail in to him.

He was on the phone and she made to put the opened correspondence on the desk in front of him and walk away, but when she did, he reached out and clasped her hand in his, preventing her from walking away. The instant he touched her she flinched, and saw the corresponding frown that crept between his brows as she did so. Anna gave an experimental tug but he continued to hold her firm.

The touch of his fingers on her skin was torture. How many times had those same fingers traversed the length of her body and wrought pleasure from her such as she had never known before? She bit back the sound that threatened to rise in her chest at the memory. The memory of the passion and the betrayal.

Finally, Judd finished his call and relinquished his hold on her.

"Get your bag, we're going to the hospital," he said in a voice that brooked no argument.

"Is Charles all right?" she asked, fear clawing at her throat at the serious expression on Judd's face.

"He's come out of the coma and he's asking for us. Both of us."

The journey to the hospital seemed to take forever, or maybe it just seemed that way because she was bound in this small space inside Judd's car. She was intensely aware of him, from the grip of his hands on the steering wheel to the set of his jaw. And his scent—the scent that insidiously reminded her of dark nights when all she knew was the feel and smell of him, and the sensation of her own pleasure, as he made love to her all through those nights.

She let out a sigh of relief as they pulled into the hospital parking lot and strived to keep her distance from Judd as they walked together to the elevator bank that would take them to the intensive-care unit.

"Only one at a time and only for five minutes," the nurse instructed.

"You go first," Judd said to Anna. "I know how important he is to you, how worried you've been."

She silently examined his words, searching for a hidden meaning behind them, but there was nothing about his expression that suggested his words meant anything other than what was said. She nodded her acquiescence and went into the room where Charles was hooked up to all manner of equipment. He opened his eyes as she entered, a shaky smile on his lips.

"Oh, Charles," she said, sinking onto the visitor's chair beside his bed, tears filling her eyes, "we've been so worried about you."

"Ah, Anna, still fussing?"

He reached for her and she gave him her hand, surprised at the strength she felt in his fingers as he squeezed tight.

"Of course I'm still fussing. I wouldn't be me if I didn't, right?"

He sighed and smiled a little wider. "That's my girl. How are things between you and my boy? Before this little incident I was beginning to hope there was something special growing between you."

Anna didn't want to talk about her and Judd, not now. "Hardly a little incident, Charles. You have to take better care of yourself. In fact, when you go home I've arranged for nursing care for you until you're back on your feet."

Her voice trailed away as she realized what she'd just said. If Cynthia Wilson had her way, Charles wouldn't be returning to the home he knew and loved. In fact, if what she'd said last Friday night held any truth to it, Charles had nowhere to call home at all. The news would shatter his chances at recovery. Somehow she had to persuade Judd to allow his father to live out his years under the roof that had been his home for over thirty years. She felt sick at the prospect but fought to keep her fears from her face. As ill as Charles was, he'd always been pretty astute. He'd know something was wrong if she didn't control herself.

"Pshaw!" he scoffed. "Nurses. I've only been awake a few hours and I've already had my fill of them. But you're not answering my question. You and Judd. What's happening there?"

"We're working well together," Anna hedged.

"Working well together." He said the words as if they tasted like something nasty. "Sounds like you've had a lovers' spat, hmm? You know, I hope you two can work out whatever it is that's keeping you apart. I know you haven't exactly had the best of role models for long-term commitment—Lord only knows I didn't treat your mother as well as I ought to have. She stood by me, you know. She held me together and loved me even when I didn't deserve it. I owed her more than companionship, but I wasn't capable of offering her more."

"Mum was happy, Charles, really." Tears pricked at Anna's eyes.

"Ah, always the mediator. You deserve more than I gave her, Anna. It's your due. Remember that."

Out the corner of her eye she saw the nurse gesture to her. "Look, my five minutes is up and I don't want to use up Judd's time with you, too. We can talk about this later."

Much later, like never, she hoped as she leaned forward to give him a chaste kiss on his cheek.

"Seemed like a very quick five minutes to me," Charles grumbled.

"I'll be back tomorrow, okay?"

"Tonight. Come back tonight."

"If I can," she promised. "Now do as you're told while you're here. Promise me?"

He merely grunted. As she passed Judd in the doorway

she took care not to brush against him, a fact that wasn't to-tally lost on Judd, judging by the expression on his face.

"I'll wait for you downstairs," she said, desperate for some air.

"Sit, sit." Charles gestured to the chair beside his bed.

Judd did as he was told. His relief at seeing Charles alert again was palpable, but even he couldn't answer himself as to why. Was it because he wanted his father to be fully aware of the payback he had coming to him, or was it something else?

"What, nothing to say?" Charles asked with a bark of laughter.

"I'm glad to see you're feeling better," Judd said stiffly.

Charles snorted. "I'll accept that, it's probably all I de-serve. There's one thing about facing your own mortality. It makes you want to clear away the messes you've made of your life—and believe me, I've made a few."

"It's how we deal with the messes that's most important," Judd replied, fighting to keep his voice neutral. Did his father plan to apologize? Did he think that saying "sorry" would make everything okay?

"That's why I needed to speak to you now. You need to know the truth about your mother and me."

"I think I know enough," Judd said, stonewalling.

"No, you don't know the half of it. I will admit it was my fault our marriage failed. I knew what I was getting into by marrying someone so much younger than me, I knew she de-served more than an older man could offer." Charles sighed and lapsed into silence.

Judd shifted uncomfortably on his chair, waiting for the older man to finish what he wanted to say. He didn't have to wait too long.

"I won't beat around the bush, my boy. I wasn't man enough for her. Now don't go getting all embarrassed. I know kids don't want to hear about their parents' sex lives." He made a self-conscious grimace. "I promise to keep it PG. Do you know much about diabetes?"

"Not a huge amount, no."

"Mine went undiagnosed for many years—part of the reason I'm here now. But one of the issues I suffer with the disease is impotence. I was thirty-five when I married your mother and I was already beginning to have problems. She was only nineteen when I met her and such a beauty. I wanted to offer her the moon and the stars. I was prepared to give her anything just to keep her. But when I started having problems in the bedroom I was ashamed. I didn't want to talk to anyone about it—not her, not my best friend, not my doctor, no one. I just threw myself into work. By the time Nicole came along we were barely sleeping together anymore.

"I just kept on working, kept on providing for Cynthia. She had the house, she had you and your sister. I just went on, hoping against hope it would be enough to keep her. She wasn't happy, but I didn't know what I could do to change that anymore. Your mother and my best friend always did get on, and Thomas seemed to be hell-bent on cheering Cynthia up. I got jealous. Started to suspect them of having an affair, of both of them cheating on me.

"One day I came home from work early. Thomas had already left the office and I found him in your mother's room, holding her, as if they were about to make love. I accused them of all sorts of things. I didn't listen when they tried to explain. Turns out she was desperately unhappy and he was consoling her, but I didn't see it that way at the time. I lost a helluva lot that day. My wife, my best friend, my son."

"You didn't have to send us away," Judd said bitterly. "She wasn't unfaithful to you, was she?"

"No," Charles acknowledged, his voice so soft Judd had to lean forward to hear him clearly. "She wasn't. But she let me believe she had been. She told me you were Thomas's child.

That she and Thomas had been having an affair for years and how much he satisfied her. She knew exactly how to hit me where it would hurt the most.

"You know the rest. I could barely see, I was so angry. I told her she could go and take you with her. I never wanted to see either of you again. When Thomas heard what I'd done, he tried to reason with me, to get me to believe the truth, but Cynthia's lies were already rotting my heart and my mind. I wouldn't listen and we never spoke again.

"He died just over a year ago. He'd arranged for his lawyers to pass on a letter to me, should he predecease me. A letter where he told me what an idiot I'd been and how he'd never touched Cynthia, ever. I knew that if he was telling the truth I'd wasted twenty-five years on a hatred I'd had no right to feel. I had to know the truth, but it took a warning from my doctors about my health before I actually found the courage to reach out to you—to admit I was wrong. It wasn't an easy thing."

Judd didn't know what to say. Everything his father told him made sense. Instinctively he knew, even though he didn't want to believe it was the truth, that Cynthia was quite capable of being so spiteful as to spin out a lie of such enormous proportions. But why had she allowed it to go on for so long? Why had she been prepared to walk away from her marriage? And had she never considered, ever, what it had meant to him to be rejected by his father—for his sister to grow up without a mother?

"Judd." Charles shifted and reached a hand toward him. Judd took it, intensely aware of the papery texture of his father's hand and remembering a time when it was strong and warm as it guided him the first time he'd ridden his bike without training wheels. "I want you to know I'm sorry, son. So very sorry for everything I put you through. I was an inflexible, prideful fool. I can't get back what I threw away, but I hope that now you know the truth you can find it in your heart to forgive me and that maybe we can start anew from here."

Judd felt unexpected moisture prick at his eyes. Every wish he'd ever had was here before him. His father was reaching out, wanting to make amends for the past. Charles had talked about his own bitterness being a waste of the last twenty-five years, but what of Judd's own? Channeling his own anger against his father for so long had been just as destructive as his father's toward Cynthia and Thomas Jackson.

"Is that why you offered me the controlling share in the company as well as the house? To make it up to me? Did you really think that would be enough?"

Charles nodded. "I hoped so. I knew you were already successfully running The Masters'. I had to sweeten the bait to bring you home—where you belong. I thought that once you were here that we could start to build a bridge between the past and now. To learn to be father and son again."

He'd come so close to throwing it all away. To destroying everything his father had worked so hard to build.

"Thank you for telling me. It's a lot to take in after all this time. I've been very angry at you for most of my life."

"I deserved that. Are you still angry?"

"Yes, but it's different now—there's more regret than anger. Frustration, too. I just wish things could have been different."

"They can be. We can make it so."

"Yes," Judd said, squeezing his father's hand gently. "Yes, Dad. We can."

By the time Judd joined Anna downstairs she felt as if she had herself back under control, externally at least. He'd been with his father for quite a while longer than she'd expected.

"What did you think?" she asked as they walked back to the car.

"He's a tough old bird. I reckon he'll be around for a few more years yet."

"Did the nurse say anything to you about when he could go home? Supposing he has a home to go to, of course."

Darn, she could probably have handled that better, she thought. But it was too late now. The words hung between them like an invisible challenge.

"What makes you think he doesn't?"

She looked at him in disbelief. "You're kidding me, right? Cynthia and Charles under one roof? She'll never allow it."

"What she will and won't allow isn't an issue," Judd said firmly as they reached the car.

"She seems to believe it is."

"Well, there's a lot that people believe at the moment. Not all of it is true," he said.

His vagueness pushed Anna to speak again. "Are you saying that Cynthia lied to me on Friday night? That it wasn't your intention to turf Charles out and install your mother back where she so supremely believes she belongs?"

"I'm not admitting or denying anything. Charles will have a home to go to—that's all you need to worry about for now."

Anna lapsed into silence, frustrated by Judd's stonewalling tactics. They were nearing their office block before she spoke again.

"I'm going to look for another job. I can't work with you. Not now. Not knowing what you're really like."

"That's your choice, but do you really think the timing is right to leave just now? Without Charles and Nicole, you're pretty much it for historical knowledge and continuity around the place. Anyone would think you want to see Wilson Wines collapse into dust."

"That's not fair. You can't expect me to keep working with you, not now that we—"

"Not now that we what, Anna?"

"Nothing."

"And your resignation?"

"I will wait until Charles is better. That's all I'm promising for now."

The thought of leaving Wilson Wines, the only job she'd ever known, terrified her. But she couldn't continue there, working for Judd, seeing him every day. Wanting him every minute.

Fourteen

Judd's head was reeling. The last thing he needed to deal with right now was Anna walking out on him. If anything, he needed her back home where she belonged as well, but he knew he had some hard work to do in that department before she'd even consider it.

What occupied his mind first and foremost now was something else. Something that challenged every belief he'd grown up with. Logically he'd always known there were two sides to every story, but he'd never dreamed his father's side of things could be so different to what he'd always been told. He'd wanted to refute the words that had poured from his father's mouth, but the man was virtually on his deathbed. Charles had no reason to lie and even with what Judd had always held to be the truth, there was a ring of honesty to what his father had said that demanded he give his old man full justice.

He couldn't concentrate on his work in the office and surprised Anna by telling her he was leaving for the day.

"Call me at the house if you need me."

"I won't," she said bluntly.

He could only give an ironic smile in response. Tough to do when what he really wanted was to lean across her desk and kiss her so thoroughly she would forget what day of the week it was. He'd save that for another time, though. Right now, he had more pressing business to attend to.

Fifteen minutes later, as he pulled into the driveway, he stopped and stared at the massive stone structure that dominated the property. He shook his head. It was only a building—yet it was so coveted, and at what cost? He eased his foot off the brake and slowly drove up the driveway. A van was parked near the front door and he pulled up alongside it, frowning as he read the lettering on the side. Decorators? He shook his head as he got out of the car and let himself in through the front door.

He could hear Cynthia in the salon and the softer murmur of another woman's voice answering her. When he opened the salon door, both women looked up, his mother's face wreathing in a smile of welcome.

"Judd, you're home early! What a lovely surprise. Here, you can tell me what you think of these." Spread before her were a stack of open books of decorating samples and she picked up a selection from the top, handing them toward him. "I think these will be perfect in here, don't you?"

"No, I don't," he said grimly before turning to the other woman. "I'm sorry, but it seems my mother has wasted your time. We won't be needing any decorating advice at the moment. Let me see you out."

The other woman looked shocked, but to her credit she hastily gathered her samples in her arms, shooting worried glances between Judd and his mother as she did so.

Cynthia sat in mutinous silence, her dark brows drawn in a straight line—a harbinger of her temper. She would never argue with him in front of a stranger but he had no doubt that her blood pressure was rising to monumental proportions right now. If there was one thing his mother hated, it was being thwarted in her goals.

Let her be angry, he thought. It was nothing compared to how he was feeling right now. By the time he'd shown the decorator out and returned to the salon, his body was rigid with tension.

"How could you do that to me, and in front of a total stranger?" She rose to her feet and demanded the instant he'd closed the door behind him.

"You're getting ahead of yourself," he said calmly. Strangely enough, in the face of her fury, he began to feel himself settle down by degrees. "The house is still mine."

"Don't you dare tell me after all this time you're changing your mind. This house is mine by right, it always has been. I just bet it's that upstart, Anna Garrick. Has she been poisoning your mind all morning? That type will always try, you know. They cloud your judgment with sexual favors and then they try to pull your strings for the rest of your life."

"Is that what you tried to do with Charles?" he asked pointedly.

Slap! In all his life his mother had never struck him, but it appeared he'd crossed a line with her today. Judd tested his stinging jaw and locked his gaze with hers.

"Now that's out of the way, perhaps you could answer my question."

"How dare you!"

"No, Mother, how dare you lie to me all these years. What kind of mother lies about her son's paternity and deliberately keeps a boy from his father?"

"Whatever I did, I did for you, Judd. *I love you.*"

"Inasmuch as you're capable of loving anyone more than you love yourself, and this house."

"You don't understand."

"Oh, I think I do. I understand you were young and foolish when you met Charles and that you saw in him a chance to relive the former Masters glory that you had pined for all your life." He shook his head. "Why did you lie to him, Mother? Why did you let him drive us away? Was it really worth hurting him so badly?"

"We'd grown apart. After I had Nicole it was as if he lost all interest in me as a woman. At first he said he was having to work longer hours and didn't want to disturb me, but then it became another excuse, and then another until we weren't even sharing a room anymore."

Judd knew his mother better than probably anyone else, and he knew that, for Cynthia, losing Charles's attentions would have been a dreadful blow to her self-esteem. For a woman who appeared so strong, she was more fragile than others knew. She measured herself by the success around her. If the physical side of her marriage was failing, then *she* was a failure.

"Why did you lie to him about Thomas Jackson?"

"You know about Thomas?"

"Only Charles's side. Now I want to hear yours. The truth this time."

His mother began to pace the room, every now and then stopping to finger one ornament or another.

"You don't know what it was like. Charles was such a dashing man when he came to visit us at The Masters' that time. And he was clearly smitten with me. The age gap didn't seem ridiculous to me—he was such a charismatic and *vital* man. He promised me everything I'd ever wanted. He promised me this." She flung her arms out wide before wrapping them tight around her middle. "He made me feel as if his entire world revolved around me. But then, he started pulling away.

"I didn't know what to do or where to turn. I had no other family here. He was my everything, and suddenly he didn't want me anymore. I just wanted to make him jealous. To make him want *me* again. So, I turned to someone else for attention, to show him that if he didn't want me, another man would."

"But his best friend? What were you thinking?"

"I wasn't thinking, that much is quite obvious. Thomas could see there was a growing rift between Charles and me. He loved us both and wanted to do whatever he could to help us over our rough patch, as he called it. I, shamefully, took advantage of his friendship and used it against him. I just wanted to hurt Charles any way I could at that point. I didn't realize then just how much I would end up hurting everyone else. When Charles threatened to send me back to Australia alone, I overreacted. I couldn't lose you and Nicole as well as my home and my marriage. I lied to him about Thomas being my lover and I led Charles to believe it was Thomas who was your father."

Cynthia sighed deeply and sank into a nearby chair. A glance at her face told of the toll her honesty had taken on her after all these years of perpetuating a lie.

Judd chose his words carefully. "They never spoke again, did you know that? Charles refused to see or speak to Thomas for the rest of his life, despite his best friend's repeated entreaties. You destroyed their friendship as thoroughly as if you really had slept with Thomas Jackson. It was only when Thomas died recently that Charles began to wonder if Thomas had really been telling the truth all along."

She nodded and wiped an errant tear from one eye. Judd wasn't moved by her unexpected emotional display. He wasn't even convinced it was genuine until she looked up and met the censure in his eyes. For the first time she showed every one of her fifty-one years and then some.

"I've been such a fool. I was so angry and so bitter it was easier to perpetuate the lie than it was to tell the truth. Besides, once Charles had it in his head that you weren't his, he couldn't wait to see the back of us. I hit him where it hurt the hardest, and he got me right back."

"You could have told him the truth at any time."

"I couldn't. I wanted him to hurt, to know what it was like to be rejected."

"He never rejected you, Mother."

"Really?" She shook her head at him. "Then what do you call him removing himself from my bed, my whole life, the way he did? If that's not rejection, then what is it?"

She stood opposite him, so proud and defiant and yet still hurting inside after all these years.

"Charles is diabetic. At that stage his illness was undiagnosed and untreated. He had no idea that's why he'd become impotent until years after, but he was too proud to seek help for the problem."

She drew in a shaky breath. "You mean it wasn't me all along?"

Cynthia's voice broke as genuine tears began to fall down her cheeks. Despite her focus still being so self-oriented, Judd felt his earlier anger toward his mother defuse entirely. He could begin to understand how her need for payback had molded her ambitious nature into one of harshness—even cruelty. She hadn't been solely responsible for what had happened; both his parents had their crosses to bear, but maybe now they could begin to heal some of the hurt they'd caused. It was going to be a monumental task. So many years and words lay like an echoing chasm between them all. He'd had enough of it. It was time for change—for all of them. Charles, Cynthia, Anna and himself.

He took a step toward his mother and drew her into his arms. Forgiveness had to start with a first step; he only hoped that he could begin to make things right before it was too late.

Judd and his mother talked for hours. When she was finally spent, he saw her to her bedroom with a light meal on a tray and went to his own room to change. She'd agreed to go back to Adelaide in the morning. She would definitely be back, but at a time when emotions weren't so fraught and when Charles was better. Who knew, perhaps between the two of them, his parents could finally lay old ghosts to rest and find some peace between them.

What a freaking day it had been. Exhaustion pulled at every part of his body. Whoever said that the truth will set you free never once mentioned the high emotional toll that could take. Today's revelations had taught him a very important lesson. Life was too short to let go of what mattered to you, especially of what you loved. He didn't want to live the rest of his life plagued by bitterness and regret over relationships he'd allowed to fall apart, as his parents had. He grabbed his cell phone from on top of his briefcase on the bed and punched in Anna's number.

She didn't pick up. No problem, he decided as he descended the stairs and headed for his car. He could ring her and ring her until she eventually gave up and answered. He knew she wouldn't turn off her phone altogether because she was one of the emergency contacts for the hospital.

"What?" she demanded as he called for the ninth time.

"Where are you? We need to talk."

"We have nothing to say."

"Yes, Anna, we do. We have everything to say to each other. I won't give up, you know. I will call you and call you until you give in."

"Look, I'm tired. Can't this wait until tomorrow at the office?"

"I need to see you now. Please? It's important."

He heard her sigh before she answered, "Fine, then."

She rattled off an address that he rapidly keyed into the GPS of the late-model Mercedes he'd bought so Evans would be free to drive Charles whenever he needed him.

"I'll be there in half an hour," he said, checking the ETA on the screen.

"Don't rush on my account," she answered before severing their connection.

By the time he pulled into the budget motel at the address Anna had given him, he felt a knot of anticipation grow tight in his gut. He parked beside her Lexus, which was outside one of the motel units that formed an L-shape just back from the road. Her door opened as he got out of his car.

"Why here?" he asked as he walked the short distance to her door.

"Clean, cheap and close to the motorway. Is that all you wanted?"

She didn't so much as budge from the doorway, nor did she seem to be in a hurry to invite him inside.

"No, that's not all I wanted."

"Then please say what you wanted to say and leave."

Anna's grip on the edge of the door made her fingers ache but she had to hold on to something, anything. If she didn't, she was afraid she might reach out to Judd, to touch him, and then she'd be lost. As much as he'd hurt her, she couldn't deny her body's response to him.

"I'm not doing this outside on the forecourt of some tacky motel, Anna. Let me in."

He spoke quietly but she had no doubt that he meant every word he said.

"If it means I'll be rid of you sooner, then, sure, come on in," she said with false bravado.

She pushed the door open wide and held her breath as he stepped over the lintel and into the compact unit she'd inhabited for the past three nights.

"Can we sit down, please?" Judd asked.

She gestured to the saggy two-seater sofa and settled herself on one of the scarred wooden chairs from the small dinette. His rangy body filled the sofa, making her all too aware of his presence in the shabby room.

"Well?" she prompted, really wanting to get this over with as soon as possible.

"I had an ulterior motive when I came to New Zealand. For years my father had spurned my mother and me, and for years I'd dreamed of what I would do if I had the opportunity to pay him back for all the heartache he'd caused when he sent us away." He paused and rubbed his jawline with a thumb and forefinger of one hand. "I should have known as I grew older that nothing is as straightforward as it seems."

"Nothing ever really is," Anna agreed, wondering where he was leading with this.

She knew he had an ulterior motive for coming to New Zealand, a motive that included turning his own flesh and blood out of his home and installing a woman whose vitriol had flayed strips off Anna's soul. Well, for all Cynthia's subtle viciousness, she'd opened Anna's eyes to the man Judd really was. She should thank her for it one day, she thought with self-deprecating irony.

"No, you're right. Nothing ever really is. My plans were originally twofold. One, to give my mother back the home she deserved, the other to ruin Wilson Wines by selling my shares to its biggest competitor."

Anna gasped. "You can't be serious! It will break Charles's heart. How could you even think of doing such a thing? How could you be so calculating?"

"Calculating? Do you have any idea of what it was like to grow up knowing your father *hated* you so much he sent you away forever? I was six years old!"

Anna recoiled as he abruptly rose to his feet and paced the small room, pushing a hand through his hair. On seeing her face, he sat back down on the sofa.

"Anna, relax. I've already begun to question what I'd planned to do with the business. Aside from the fact that I'd been bored with my work in Adelaide for some time, working at Wilson Wines has provided me with new challenges within the industry that make me very excited for the future of the company—not to mention valuable insights into how hard Charles has worked to keep the business running all these years. If nothing else, I learned to respect him for that.

"Look, I don't expect anyone to think that my plans were honorable—revenge very rarely is. But I've both learned and been forced to face some home truths about my parents and myself that have turned everything upside down."

"I don't see what any of this has to do with me. Why are you telling me?" Anna clenched her fingers together in her lap.

"Because you were part of that revenge."

Fifteen

A bitter taste flooded her mouth. She'd heard as much from Cynthia, but hearing the words directly from lips that she'd kissed in deepest passion, lips that had caressed her entire body and brought her ultimate pleasure, made her stomach lurch. She shot up from her seat.

"I think I've heard enough. I'd like you to go."

Judd stood and reached for her, his fingers closing around her upper arms and gently encouraging her back down on her chair.

"No, you haven't heard nearly enough, and I won't leave until you know it all."

"I don't want to hear it, Judd. You hurt me so much it pains me to see you at work every day. I can't keep putting myself through this. I don't deserve to be made to feel this way."

"No, you don't, and that's why I'm going to make it up to you. Look, when I met you I was instantly attracted to you. That attraction was definitely mutual, as we both established on your first night at The Masters'. But it wasn't until the next morning when my mother told me that she'd figured out who you were that I made a decision to use that attraction against you.

"You see, I had no reason to believe that you weren't there as Charles's puppet. You were so loyal to him, so defensive. It made me wonder just how deep the relationship between the two of you went. I assumed, wrongly I know, that the two of you were lovers, and to add to my revenge plans I wanted to win you off him. To show him that he didn't deserve to be loved the way you obviously loved him."

A tiny sound of pain emerged from Anna's mouth. She'd known that Judd had thought she was Charles's lover, but to hear him put in words what he'd been thinking hit her like a physical blow. She wrapped her hands around her stomach and hunched over as if by doing so she could protect herself from what he insisted on saying.

"Anna, I'm so sorry I treated you like that, and I hope that you'll be able to forgive me. I based my need for vengeance on a life that was as orchestrated as what I'd planned to do to my father. Granted, he's no angel, but he didn't deserve what I had planned to do."

A difficult silence fell between them, a silence punctuated by nothing more than the overloud hum of the old refrigerator and the ticking of the cheap plastic wall clock. Finally, Anna summoned up the courage to ask him the one question that now burned inside her.

"So what changed your mind?"

"You."

He looked up and his eyes burned a hole straight to her heart. Anna swallowed against the fear that formed a lump in her throat.

"You'll forgive me if I say I find that hard to believe."

He gave a humorless laugh. "I don't blame you, but it's true. In everything around me, you are the only thing that's good. You're the only one who remained true to the people you love. I learned today that the truth I'd always believed growing up was nothing but a lie fabricated by one person's need for attention and another's pride standing in the way of giving it."

"What do you mean?" Anna asked, suddenly confused.

A stricken look of pain settled on Judd's face. "My mother lied to me for most of my life. Forcing the truth from her today was one of the hardest things I've had to endure."

"But how did you know she'd lied to you?"

"Charles told me his side of their story today at the hospital. It was the bare-bones version, given how weak he is and how much time we were allowed together, but it made me stop seeing him as the villain in the piece and start to see him as he is. Faults as well as strengths. I knew he had accused my mother of having an affair. She told me that much when I was about fifteen. What she didn't say was that she'd deliberately led him to believe it, then told him I wasn't his son." He shook his head. "And to think I was prepared to crush him without knowing all of that.

"I can't believe I almost threw everything away. Everything—everyone—I'd ever wanted in my life were mine all along, if only I'd had the courage to fight for them. Learning the truth was a real eye-opener for me."

"What you were going to do was despicable. What you did, to me, was despicable."

"I know, and I'm more sorry for that than you'll ever know. It seems betrayal runs in the family. My mother lied to Charles about my paternity in retaliation for what she saw as his indifference to her. She had no idea that what she perceived as his coolness toward her masked a bigger problem."

Anna caught on quickly. "His diabetes. My mother said he'd probably had it for years before he was diagnosed."

"Yes, he was too proud and too embarrassed to seek help, and so frightened that he would lose his beautiful young wife because of it that he poured himself into work so he could at least keep her in the lifestyle he'd always promised her.

"I learned some awful truths about my family today, Anna. Not least of which were the truths about myself. Truths I'm so bitterly ashamed of. I want to make it up to you, if you'll allow me. Everyone deserves a second chance, right? A chance to put things back the way they should have been all along?"

"I don't know if I can do that, Judd. All my life I watched my mother be treated as an afterthought, appreciated to an extent but never really given the love she craved. She deserved more than that—so much more—and so do I. From an early age I told myself that I would only be with someone who loved me completely and put our relationship first.

"When I realized what you thought of me, why you had sex with me," she said bluntly, because no matter how engaged her feelings it could only have been sex, not lovemaking, "I felt second-rate. Your revenge came first, not me. I don't know if I can forgive you that. I really don't."

Judd reached across the short distance between them and took her hands in his, his thumbs stroking across the tops of hers.

"I love you, Anna. I never thought I'd want to trust another person the way I want to trust you. With my mother's lies about my father poisoning the way I saw love, I never wanted to go through what I thought was the greatest weakness in the world. Allowing yourself to become vulnerable to another person, to hand to them the means to hurt you so much, alters the entire course of your life. But I want to be that vulnerable to you. I trust you. I know you. You are loyal and loving and everything I was never taught to be. I would do anything for you, and I swear that from now on I will always put you first. Please, let me show you that I love you."

Anna lifted her head and met his intense and pleading gaze. Her heart wanted to say yes to him, but her head cau-

tioned her to take care. She'd suffered so much these past
weeks. Yes, she'd experienced the highest of highs in her
life, but along with those came the lows to which she never
wanted to descend again.

She took a deep breath. "So, if I asked you to show me you
love me by leaving me now, by never talking to me again, by
never making another attempt to see me, you'd do it?"

She saw the pain that speared across his features, the light
in his eyes dim as he saw all hope of their reconciliation
being dashed against his mistakes of the past. Judd let her
go and stood up.

"Yes," he said. "I will do that for you."

His hands were trembling and it shocked Anna to her core
that his emotions affected him so deeply. Judd Wilson, the
ice man, vulnerable to her.

Before he could reach the door of the unit, she flew to her
feet.

"Judd! Stop!"

She ran toward him, throwing herself against his back and
flinging her arms around him as if she could physically stop
him from leaving her.

"Don't go, please don't go. I love you, Judd. Don't ever
walk away from me again, please?"

He turned in her arms, wrapping his own around her and
holding her close. As she looked up at his face she saw tears
tracking down his cheeks. She lifted shaking hands to wipe
the moisture away.

"Oh, Judd, don't."

She drew his head down to hers, sealing his mouth with
her lips and putting her heart into her kiss, telling him how
much he meant to her with actions rather than words.

"God, don't do that to me again. I couldn't survive it another time," he groaned against her mouth.

Suddenly she understood just what it had cost Judd to walk
away from her like that. He'd been a confused little boy when

his father had cast him off like a forgotten and unwanted piece of his life. By his own admission he hadn't learned to love or to trust easily, and he'd given her his heart, laid all his truths on the line for her. Her happiness came first with him, she knew that now.

"I won't. I won't ever send you away from me and I won't ever leave you again, I promise."

She kissed him again before taking his hands and leading him to the bedroom. It was small, it was basic, but it was all she needed as the stage to show him how very important he was to her.

He didn't move so much as a muscle as she undressed. His eyes, however, tracked her movements as avidly as a child watching the presents under the tree at Christmas. When she was naked, she reached for his sweater and pulled it over his head before reaching for his belt and the button fly of his jeans. Goose bumps raised on her skin as she looked her fill of this beautiful man who'd laid his heart on the line for her, but they had nothing to do with a chill in the air.

She stepped into him, at first wrapping her arms around his waist and feeling the heat of him seep into her—skin to skin, head to toe. Then she turned her face into him and traced a line of gentle kisses across his chest before taking his hand again and leading him to the bed. She yanked down the covers, exposing the crisp white cotton sheets, and pushed him onto the mattress with a smile that spoke of all the things she wanted to do with him.

Judd's pupils dilated, consuming the blue of his irises, as she straddled his legs and began to gently stroke his body with a feather-light touch that made his skin jump and heat beneath the soft pads.

"I love you, Judd Wilson," she whispered against his skin as she lowered her mouth to repeat the trail her fingers had taken, and punctuated each word with a press of her lips.

"I love you, too, Anna Garrick. I want to marry you. I want to do this right. Will you be my wife?"

"Judd, you don't need to marry me. I know how you feel about your parents' marriage. I don't need a formal union to know you love me."

Judd reached for her and rolled with her, tucking her body beneath him. He cradled her head between his hands.

"I mean it, Anna, I want to do right by you. I want to spend the rest of my life with you, make babies with you and raise those babies to be wonderful people. People who know their parents are right there behind them, through everything."

"Are you sure, Judd? We can do all that without marrying."

"I know, but I *want* to marry you. I want the world to hear my pledge to you and to know that you will be mine for all time."

Anna lay beneath him, feeling the warmth of him, the strength of him, the passion within him, and she knew she wanted it, too. She raised a hand to trace the lines of his beautiful face, letting her fingers settle on his lips as she reached her decision.

"Yes," she answered tremulously. "Yes, I'd be proud to be your wife."

"Thank you." He rested his forehead on hers and closed his eyes. Anna could feel the tension easing from his body. "I will make sure there is not a day that goes by that you regret it."

"I'll hold you to that," she said with a soft smile.

And then words were redundant as they showed one another the reaches of the physical manifestation of their love. Anna cradled him with her body, her legs parting to allow him to nestle at the core of her. She felt the blunt tip of him nudge at her opening, felt him slide inside. She tightened around him, welcoming his possession. Judd raised himself slightly, his eyes locked with hers as he began to move, at first slowly and then with increasing rhythm, never once losing focus.

Pleasure began to build inside of her but it was different than before. This time they were so much more connected—mind, body and spirit. And when she began to shake with the intensity of her orgasm, she felt him tremble also until with a raw cry he spilled himself within her. Making love had never felt so right or so perfect. A tear slid from the corner of her eye as emotion overwhelmed her.

He was her man, her love, her forever. And she was his.

* * * * *

PASSION

For a spicier, decidedly hotter read—
this is your destination for romance!

COMING NEXT MONTH
AVAILABLE MARCH 13, 2012

#2143 TEMPTED BY HER INNOCENT KISS
Pregnancy & Passion
Maya Banks

#2144 BEHIND BOARDROOM DOORS
Dynasties: The Kincaids
Jennifer Lewis

#2145 THE PATERNITY PROPOSITION
Billionaires and Babies
Merline Lovelace

#2146 A TOUCH OF PERSUASION
The Men of Wolff Mountain
Janice Maynard

**#2147 A FORBIDDEN
AFFAIR**
The Master Vintners
Yvonne Lindsay

**#2148 CAUGHT IN
THE SPOTLIGHT**
Jules Bennett

HDCNM0212

REQUEST YOUR FREE BOOKS!
2 FREE NOVELS PLUS 2 FREE GIFTS!

Harlequin *Desire*

ALWAYS POWERFUL, PASSIONATE AND PROVOCATIVE

YES! Please send me 2 FREE Harlequin Desire® novels and my 2 FREE gifts (gifts are worth about $10). After receiving them, if I don't wish to receive any more books, I can return the shipping statement marked "cancel." If I don't cancel, I will receive 6 brand-new novels every month and be billed just $4.30 per book in the U.S. or $4.99 per book in Canada. That's a saving of at least 14% off the cover price! It's quite a bargain! Shipping and handling is just 50¢ per book in the U.S. and 75¢ per book in Canada.* I understand that accepting the 2 free books and gifts places me under no obligation to buy anything. I can always return a shipment and cancel at any time. Even if I never buy another book, the two free books and gifts are mine to keep forever.

225/326 HDN FEF3

Name _____ (PLEASE PRINT)

Address _____ Apt. #

City _____ State/Prov. _____ Zip/Postal Code

Signature (if under 18, a parent or guardian must sign)

Mail to the **Reader Service:**

IN U.S.A.: P.O. Box 1867, Buffalo, NY 14240-1867
IN CANADA: P.O. Box 609, Fort Erie, Ontario L2A 5X3

Not valid for current subscribers to Harlequin Desire books.

Want to try two free books from another line?
Call 1-800-873-8635 or visit www.ReaderService.com.

* Terms and prices subject to change without notice. Prices do not include applicable taxes. Sales tax applicable in N.Y. Canadian residents will be charged applicable taxes. Offer not valid in Quebec. This offer is limited to one order per household. All orders subject to credit approval. Credit or debit balances in a customer's account(s) may be offset by any other outstanding balance owed by or to the customer. Please allow 4 to 6 weeks for delivery. Offer available while quantities last.

Your Privacy—The Reader Service is committed to protecting your privacy. Our Privacy Policy is available online at www.ReaderService.com or upon request from the Reader Service.

We make a portion of our mailing list available to reputable third parties that offer products we believe may interest you. If you prefer that we not exchange your name with third parties, or if you wish to clarify or modify your communication preferences, please visit us at www.ReaderService.com/consumerchoice or write to us at Reader Service Preference Service, P.O. Box 9062, Buffalo, NY 14269. Include your complete name and address.

HDES11B

New York Times *and* USA TODAY *bestselling author
Maya Banks presents book three in her miniseries*
PREGNANCY & PASSION.

TEMPTED BY HER INNOCENT KISS

Available March 2012 from Harlequin Desire!

There came a time in a man's life when he knew he was well and truly caught. Devon Carter stared down at the diamond ring nestled in velvet and acknowledged that this was one such time. He snapped the lid closed and shoved the box into the breast pocket of his suit.

He had two choices. He could marry Ashley Copeland and fulfill his goal of merging his company with Copeland Hotels, thus creating the largest, most exclusive line of resorts in the world, or he could refuse and lose it all.

Put in that light, there wasn't much he could do except pop the question.

The doorman to his Manhattan high-rise apartment hurried to open the door as Devon strode toward the street. He took a deep breath before ducking into his car, and the driver pulled into traffic.

Tonight was the night. All of his careful wooing, the countless dinners, kisses that started brief and casual and became more breathless—all a lead-up to tonight. Tonight his seduction of Ashley Copeland would be complete, and then he'd ask her to marry him.

He shook his head as the absurdity of the situation hit him for the hundredth time. Personally, he thought William Copeland was crazy for forcing his daughter down Devon's throat.

Ashley was a sweet enough girl, but Devon had no desire

to marry anyone.

William had other plans. He'd told Devon that Ashley had no head for the family business. She was too softhearted, too naive. So he'd made Ashley part of the deal. The catch? Ashley wasn't to know of it. Which meant Devon was stuck playing stupid games.

Ashley was supposed to think this was a grand love match. She was a starry-eyed woman who preferred her animal-rescue foundation over board meetings, charts and financials for Copeland Hotels.

If she ever found out the truth, she wouldn't take it well.

And hell, he couldn't blame her.

But no matter the reason for his proposal, before the night was over, she'd have no doubts that she belonged to him.

What will happen when Devon marries Ashley?
Find out in Maya Banks's passionate new novel
TEMPTED BY HER INNOCENT KISS
Available March 2012 from Harlequin Desire!

Harlequin *Presents*

USA TODAY bestselling author

Carol Marinelli

begins a daring duet.

THE SECRETS
of
XANOS

Two brothers alike in charisma and power;
separated at birth and seeking revenge…

Nico has always felt like an outsider. He's turned his back on his parents' fortune to become one of Xanos's most powerful exports and nothing will stand in his way—until he stumbles upon a virgin bride….

Zander took his chances on the streets rather than spending another moment under his cruel father's roof. Now he is unrivaled in business—and the bedroom! He wants the best people around him, and Charlotte is the best PA! Can he tempt her over to the dark side…?

A SHAMEFUL CONSEQUENCE
Available in March

AN INDECENT PROPOSITION
Available in April

HP13053